KING PENGUIN

A TIGER FOR MALGUDI

R. K. Narayan was born in Madras, South India, and educated there and at Maharaja's College in Mysore. His first novel *Swami and Friends* (1935) and its successor *The Bachelor of Arts* (1937) are both set in the enchanting fictional territory of Malgudi. Other 'Malgudi' novels are *The Dark Room* (1938), *The English Teacher* (1945), *Mr Sampath* (1949), *The Financial Expert* (1952), *The Man-Eater of Malgudi* (1961), *The Vendor of Sweets* (1967) and *The Painter of Signs* (1977); the last three are also published in Penguin. His novel *The Guide* (1958) won him the National Prize of the Indian Literary Academy, his country's highest literary honour. He was awarded in 1980 the A. C. Benson Medal by the Royal Society of Literature and in 1981 he was made an Honorary Member of the American Academy and Institute of Arts and Letters. As well as four collections of short stories, *A Horse and Two Goats*, *An Astrologer's Day and Other Stories*, *Lawley Road* and *Malgudi Days*, he has published two travel books *My Dateless Diary* and *The Emerald Route*, two collections of essays, *Next Saturday* and *Reluctant Guru*, and a volume of memoirs, *My Days*.

R. K. NARAYAN

──

A TIGER FOR
MALGUDI

A KING PENGUIN
PUBLISHED BY PENGUIN BOOKS

Penguin Books Ltd, Harmondsworth, Middlesex, England
Penguin Books, 40 West 23rd Street, New York, New York 10010, U.S.A.
Penguin Books Australia Ltd, Ringwood, Victoria, Australia
Penguin Books Canada Ltd, 2801 John Street, Markham, Ontario, Canada L3R 1B4
Penguin Books (N.Z.) Ltd, 182–190 Wairau Road, Auckland 10, New Zealand

First published in the United States of America by The Viking Press 1983
First published in Great Britain by William Heinemann Ltd 1983
Published in Penguin Books 1984

A selection from this book appeared originally
in *The Missouri Review*, and the Introduction
appeared in the *Vassar Quarterly*.

Made and printed in Great Britain by
Richard Clay (The Chaucer Press) Ltd, Bungay, Suffolk
Set in 10/12½ Monophoto Sabon

I have no idea of the extent of this zoo. I know only my corner and whatever passes before me. On the day I was wheeled in, I only noticed two gates opening to admit me. When I stood up I caught a glimpse of some cages ahead and also heard the voice of a lion. The man who had transferred me from the forest stepped out of his jeep and said, after a glance in my direction, 'He is all right. Now run up and see if the end cage is ready. This animal is used to human company and a lot of free movement. We must keep him where people will be passing. The open-air enclosure must also be available to him, when the wild ones are not let out. See to it.'

They have shown me special consideration, by the grace of my Master, whom I may not see again. All the same, lying here on the cool floor, I madly hope that my Master might suddenly appear out of a crowd, open the door of my cage, and command, 'Come out, let us go.' Such is my dream. I keep scrutinizing faces, but all faces look dull and monotonous, none radiant like my Master's. Men, women, and children peer through the bars, and sometimes cry aloud, 'Ah, see this tiger. What a ferocious beast!' and make crude noises to rouse me, fling a stone if the keeper is not looking, and move on to appreciate similarly the occupant of the next cage. You are not likely to understand that I am different from the tiger next door, that I possess a soul within this forbidding exterior. I can think, analyse, judge, remember and do everything that you can do, perhaps with greater subtlety and sense. I lack only the faculty of speech.

But if you could read my thoughts, you would be welcome to come in and listen to the story of my life. At least, you could slip your arm through the bars and touch me and I will hold out my forepaw to greet you, after retracting my claws, of course. You are carried away by appearances – my claws and fangs and the glowing eyes frighten you no doubt. I don't blame you. I don't know why God has chosen to give us this fierce make-up, the same God who has created the parrot, the peacock, and the deer, which inspire poets and painters. I would not blame you for keeping your distance – I myself shuddered at my own reflection on the still surface of a pond while crouching for a drink of water, not when I was really a wild beast, but after I came under the influence of my Master and learnt to question, 'Who am I?' Don't laugh within yourself to hear me speak thus. I'll tell you about my Master presently.

I recollect my early days as a cave-dweller and jungle beast (however much my Master might have disliked the term) with a mixture of pleasure and shame. At the far end of Mempi range, which trails off into the plains, I lived in my cave on the edge of a little rivulet, which swelled and roared along when it rained in the hills but was fordable in dry season, with the jungle stretching away on the other side. I remember my cubhood when I frolicked on the sandy bank and in the cool stream, protected and fed by a mother. I had no doubt whatever that she would live for ever to look after me: a natural delusion which afflicts all creatures, including human beings. However, she just vanished from my world one evening. I was seized with panic and hid myself in the cave. When I ventured out, I was chased, knocked down and hurt by bigger animals and menaced by lesser ones. I starved except when I could catch miserable creatures such as rabbits, foxcubs and squirrels, and survived somehow. Not only survived, but in course of time considered myself the Supreme Lord of the Jungle, afraid of no one, striking terror in others. It was, naturally, a time of utter wildness, violence, and unthinking cruelty inflicted on weaker creatures. Everyone I encountered proved weaker and submissive, but that submissiveness did not count – I delivered the fatal blow in any case when I wished and strode about as the King of the Forest. By the way, who crowned the lion King of the Forest? Probably a fable writer, carried away by the pompous mane and beard, I suppose! A more slothful creature was never created. All his energy is conserved for hunting food, and once that is accomplished he lies down for days on end, so reluctant to move a muscle that he could be used by any other jungle creature as a mattress; it would make no difference to him if birds nested in his beard and laid eggs. As for his supreme strength I had a chance to test it in the circus ring once, when we were let out to fight and he fled into a waiting cage thanking the Creator for the damage of only one ear, which came off when I tried to comb his royal mane. I got a pat on my back from the ringmaster himself.

Every creature in the jungle trembled when it sensed my approach. 'Let them tremble and understand who is the Master, Lord of this world,' I thought with pride. When I strode out from the cave, the scent went ahead, and except monkeys and birds on trees all other creatures shrank out of sight. While I prowled through, half-sunk in jungle grass, I expected the deferential withdrawal from my path of other creatures. We the denizens of the jungle can communicate, without words, exactly as human beings do – we are capable of expressing to each other sympathy, warning, abuse, irony, insult, love and hatred exactly in the manner of human beings, but only when necessary, unlike human beings who talk all their waking hours, and even in sleep. When I passed by, rabbits scurried off, and if a jackal happened to be in my path, he put his ears back, lowered his tail, rolled his eyes in humility, and cried softly: 'Here comes our Lord and Master. Keep his path clear . . .'

Such attention pleased me, and seemed to add to my stature. Occasionally I came across a recalcitrant member of our society who probably thought highly of himself and I always noted, through a corner of my eye, how he pretended not to have seen me, looking the other way or asleep behind a thorny bush out of my reach. I made a mental note of such lapses of courtesy and never failed to punish him when a chance occurred. It might not be more than a scratch or a bite while passing him the next time, but that would take days to heal, and he would lose an eye or a tooth or earn a cut on his lips making it impossible for him to eat his food, all of which I counted as a trophy. Whenever I saw the creature again, you may be sure he never displayed any arrogance. Among our jungle community, we had an understanding, which was an acknowledgement of my superiority, unquestioned, undisputed. My Master, when I mentioned it, explained that it was also true of human beings in various degrees and versions.

While all living creatures avoided me, there was one which I took great care to avoid – the porcupine, after an early experience. Out of a sort of recklessness I once tried to toss him about, and received such a stab of quills over my nose, jaws, and paws that I retreated to my cave and collapsed. I lay there starving for several days; I expected I would soon be dead. A long-tailed, black-faced langur, perched at a safe distance on the branch of a fig tree, munching fruits as the monkey tribe always do, simpered, leered, and said, 'Served you right. No one in his right mind would ever go near a porcupine. Ignorant fool. Should you run after every kind of flesh indiscriminately? You think no end of your prowess!' I looked up and growled, wishing I could reach him. (He then went out and spread the news far and wide, making it the joke of the season in the jungle.) 'Shut up,' I cried, and the long-tailed one said, 'Yes, after I have said this, you despot, now listen carefully. If you can move yourself across the stream, not far off there is a yellow shrub with bristles. Brush against it; milk from its leaves will loosen the quills and heal your sores. You see that hollow over there, go, drop yourself in it, sink down in it, roll in it; it is full of those plants . . .'

Forgive me, if you find me running into the past. Whenever I recollect my forest life, I am likely to lose all restraint. I have often felt guilty at reminiscing, but my Master, who reads my mind, has said that there is nothing wrong in it, and advises me not to curb it – it being also a part of my own life, indispensable and unshakable although I have come a long way from it. . .

I only worried about monkeys – they lived at a height and moved and ran about as they pleased, and thought they were above the normal rules and laws of the jungle, a mischievous tribe. I was aware of how they hopped from place to place, hiding amidst foliage, bearing malicious rumours and trying to damage my authority. Their allies were birds which lived at a height and enjoyed greater facility than monkeys in that they could fly away at my approach. How I longed sometimes to be able to climb or fly even a short distance. Then I would have eliminated this whole contemptible clan; I particularly wished to get at the owl, the wise one with his round eyes always looking down his hook nose, a self-appointed adviser to all those despicable creatures who secretly wished my downfall. (I'm only expressing my mentality in those days in the idiom of those times.) Every time I passed below a tree, I would hear a cynical cackle and hoot and if I looked up I'd see the loving couple, the owl and her mate. One would say to the other, 'When the King passes, what should one do?' There would be some answer to that.

'If you don't?'

'Then he will nip off your head.'

'Yes – only if he could carry his mighty bulk up a tree trunk . . .'

The crow was particularly treacherous, always following my movements and creating enough din to reveal where I had the kill, making it impossible for me to eat in peace, sneaking up to peck at my food and retreating when I turned, again and again. Worse than the crow were kites, vultures, eagles and such, which circled loftily in the high heaven, but to no greater purpose than to spot out carrion, glide down and clean it up to the bone. Mean creatures, ever on the watch for someone else's kill.

Another creature that I had my eyes on was the leopard. I don't know how many members of that odious family existed in my forest – they didn't seem to breed or multiply too openly. The leopard was so secretive that you never noticed more than one at a time and hardly ever a family. It has always been a mystery. When I passed by he would climb a tree pointedly to emphasize the fact that he was higher than myself. I tried to ignore this creature, since he possessed great agility and could get beyond anyone's reach, but he was mean, and always made it clear that he was there and didn't care for me. He made all kinds of noises while I passed, and purred and growled and sneered. When he was with his mate it was worse. They made audible remarks most insulting to a tiger, and talked among themselves about the superiority of spots over stripes.

There was a jungle superstition about how the tiger came to have stripes. The first tiger in creation was very much like a lion, endowed with a tawny, shining coat of pure gold. Imagine! But he offended some forest spirit, which branded his back with hot coal. Thus goes the fable, which I didn't believe in, a canard started by some jealous creature like the leopard who felt inferior owing to his spots, but made a virtue of it. The leopard couple sang this fable every time I passed by, a monotonous silly song; I would have put an end to their song if I could have seen where they were – they were mostly unseen, and just streaked away like lightning when glimpsed. I was helpless with this truant. It hurt my pride as a ruler of the jungle, while all other creatures respected my status, bowed to it and kept out of my way. Night and day I spent in planning and thinking how best to humble the leopard or exterminate him. Sometimes I set out to track him down in his lair, in a deep hollow or inside a cave. When I went in quest, he would invariably anticipate my arrival and sneak away, and then sit atop a steep, slippery rock, and eye me with contempt or go up a banyan tree with the ease of a squirrel ... I realized soon that I had to tolerate his existence and bide my time. This was a great worry for me. He disturbed and scared off my game and was ahead of me in hunting.

The leopard was not the last of my worries. I could ignore him and go my way. Not so a female of our species, whom I encountered beyond those mango groves — a creature as large as myself, I suppose. I smelt her presence a long way off. I hesitated whether to turn back or advance. I was out to hunt for the evening, and if I had not been hungry I would have withdrawn and gone my way in a different direction. But I was proceeding to the meadow beyond the valley where I knew a herd of deer always grazed. I noticed her sitting erect in the middle of the road blocking my passage. I'd never seen her before; probably from an adjoining forest. Normally we respected each other's territories and never intruded. My temper rose at the sight of her. 'Get out of my way and go back where you belong,' I roared. She just took it as a joke and showed no response except a slight wave of her tail. This was complete insolence and not to be tolerated. With her back to me she was watching the herd in the meadow. I was furious and jumped on her back and tried to throttle her, with the sort of hold that would make a wild buffalo limp in a second. But this lady surprised me by throwing me off her back with a jerk. My claws were buried in her skin, but that did not make any difference to her as she turned round and gashed my eyes and bit my throat. Fortunately I had shut my eyes, but my brow was torn and blood trickled down my eyes. The jackal, as always attracted by the smell of blood, was there as if summoned, hiding behind a thicket of thorns; he made his presence felt, and mumbled some advice, which was lost in the uproar the lady was creating as she returned for the attack and knocked me off my feet by ramming into me. I have never encountered anyone so strong.

Now the safest course for me would be to retreat gracefully to my cave and get away from this monster quickly. But my dignity would be lost – especially with the jackal there watching my humiliation. I should fight it out, even if one of us were to die in the process. We butted into each other, scratched, clawed, wrestled, grappled, gashing, biting, tearing each other, and I also stood up and threw my weight on her and struck, but it was like beating a rock – she was no normal animal: there is a limit to physical endurance; and I could stand it no longer; I collapsed on the ground bleeding from every pore; I had no strength even to run away, which I wished I had done earlier instead of bothering about prestige before the damned jackal. If I had seized and choked the jackal, I could have saved my blood.

In a few places my skin hung down in ribbons. My satisfaction was that the monster, my adversary, seemed to have fared no better. She had also collapsed in a ditch, no less bloody, with her flesh torn up and exposed. I noticed also that while I could open my eyes with blood dripping, she lay with her eyes swollen and sealed. I remembered aiming at her eyes just as she was trying to gouge out mine, but I seemed to have had better luck. It was her inability to open her eyes, more than physical collapse, which forced her to withdraw.

While both of us lay panting, the jackal came out of his shelter and, standing at a safe distance, raised his voice so that both of us could hear him. He knew that neither of us was in a state to go for him if we did not like his words; all the same he kept his distance and a possible retreat open. The jackal asked with an air of great humility, 'May I know why you have been fighting and brought on yourselves this misery? If you can show even half of half a reason, I shall be satisfied.' Neither of us could answer, but only moan and growl. For the condition I was in, the jackal could have patted my cheeks or pulled my whiskers and got away with it. I could at least see the world around but the tigress was blinded for the time being.

The jackal continued ingratiatingly, 'If you cannot discover a reason to be enemies, why don't you consider being friends? How grand you could make it if you joined forces – you could become supreme in this jungle and the next and the next; no one will ever try to stand up to you, except a crazy tusker, whom you could toss about between you two . . . If you combined you could make all the jungle shake.'

His words sounded agreeable. I felt a sudden compassion for my adversary and also gratitude for being spared my life. I struggled to get up on my feet and, mistaking my action, the jackal swiftly withdrew and disappeared before I could say, 'You have advised us well.' I limped along to the tigress very cautiously and expressed my contrition and desire to make amends. She was in no condition to rise or see me. I cleaned up the bloody mess covering her eyes and sat beside her huge body, paying all attention and performing many acts of tenderness – till she was able to open one eye slightly and stir, and it filled me with dread lest she should kill me instantly. She could have easily done it, if she was so disposed. But a change had come over her too. My ministrations seemed to have helped her to recover her breath, vision, and the use of her limbs. She followed me quietly, although both of us were limping, to an adjacent pond and we splashed about in the water till we were cleansed of blood and felt revived.

We have no reckoning of time in the manner of human beings. But by the time the scars on our backs were dry, a litter of four was added to our family, climbing and jumping over us all the time in the cave.

It was all very well as long as they were sucklings. At that stage they never moved away, their horizon being their mother's belly. The little ones were happy, continuously suckling, or when fully fed, climbing and jumping over their mother's immense sides as she stretched herself across the floor of our home. It left me free to

[19]

roam in the jungle and rest, away from the family. Usually I found the shade of a bamboo cluster very pleasant – I merged in its speckled shade so completely that some little buck or minor game would stray near me, and I'd only have to turn and grab in order to provide food for the cubs.

When they grew up and discovered the use of their limbs, they ran about in different directions. They were now at an unsafe stage. Any bear or bison could trample them out of existence: no reason why such a thing should happen – except that the jungle was a devilish place, where the weak or the young received no consideration for their helpless state. We had to guard them all the time. One would run in the direction of the stream, another wade through, and the third would have climbed a rock, where a colony of giant eagles nested, which might swoop down and carry him off, leaving his bones to bleach in the sun. Equally dangerous were the pythons who just swallowed whole whatever came their way. Also there was the danger of the cubs slipping and rolling down into the ravine. We had to save them from destruction every other minute. They were now too large to be carried by the scruff, and we caught and pummelled them along back into the cave, and one of us would lie across the entrance to prevent their going out again. This could be no permanent solution.

A time came when the obstacle at the cave-mouth made no difference to them. When the sentry parent was fallen into a doze, they could easily hop over him and explore the world. Though we enjoyed the spectacle of our cubs' activities, it was becoming a sore trial. It was my turn one evening to guard the cubs. Their mother had gone out in search of prey. I saw her go down the sandy slope across the river and climb the other bank. I had supposed the cubs were playing inside at the back wall of the cave. But at some moment when I was not alert enough, they must have vaulted over me and escaped. When I woke up I saw them wading across the river, their little heads bobbing above the water. I watched them go, feeling too lazy to run after them. Evidently they were following their mother's scent. No harm. I could see them go up the opposite bank; they could reach their mother and come back later. After all they had to gain experience: it'd do them good to watch their mother hunt and share a fresh kill.

The air blowing in our direction brought some strange unfamiliar noises, and crackling sounds like twigs breaking. I felt disturbed and bewildered. No sign of the cubs or the mother. I let out a roar that should ring through the forest, valleys and mountains, and summon back my family. Normally when I called there would be an answer, but today there was none – only the twittering of birds waking at dawn. I ventured out, down the sand and across the river, following the course I had watched the cubs take; the scent led me on and on to the ridge, and then down a valley to the plains which had a path leading to human habitations beyond the jungle. I cried in anguish and desperation – but silenced myself and crouched unobtrusively when I noticed far off in the valley down below a line of men passing, pulling and pushing an open cart on which were laid out the cubs and their mother. The men were singing and shouting vociferously, and did not hear my cry. I had thought till now that our jungle home was impregnable, and un-approachable for human beings. In fact, I had hardly seen any specimen till this moment. Now human feet had strayed in and touched our ground, and that brought to my mind strange fore-bodings. I watched the revellers wend their way. They were too intoxicated to notice me, since I lay concealed behind the boulders. As the procession wound along, I hopped on to another rock and stalked them. As the sun came up my eyes were dazzled, and the procession melted into thin air. I edged to the shade of an over-hanging cliff and stayed there.

I slept till dusk. I got up and moved in the direction the procession had gone. I took care not to be noticed by any jungle creature – particularly the owl or the jackal who always spied on my movements. I moved away from the trees on which the owl generally was perched and the bushes where the jackal would be sneaking around. I kept my movements along the rocks on the hill at a safe height. When I arrived at a village, I found most of the inhabitants asleep. Noiselessly I went up and lay beside a well until everything was quiet.

The cart in which the cubs and their mother were laid out was left to one side in the village street. I could see it all clearly from my hiding place. The sight of my family stretched out there filled me with fury. In those days I was still a tiger, an unmitigated animal, and the only feeling that was aroused in me was fury, rather than grief, which I understand now. A blind, impossible anger stirred within me: I just wanted to dash up, pounce upon every creature, bite and claw and destroy. I wanted to spring forward, pick up the cubs and carry them away.

Just as I was getting ready to dash up, a set of human beings arrived in a strange vehicle, which I now understand to be a jeep. They shouted and summoned the villagers. The village was astir and a crowd gathered around the cart, and there was much jabbering, arguments and shouting. I held myself back although I felt a great drive within to pounce on that whole lot and tear their entrails. But I held myself back. No one knew that I was there. I lay low, watched them transfer the carcasses to the back of their jeep, and drive off. The villagers went back to their homes; silence and darkness fell on the village. I came out of my hiding place behind the well and prowled around. Some of the street dogs started barking and woke up the villagers again. Before they could notice me, I withdrew and went back to my hiding place beside the well. Even there I could not stay too long. Women started approaching the well carrying pots and buckets and chattering among themselves; I slipped back and hid myself on the hill behind *lantana* bushes.

Another day's sun came up, and I dozed off till the evening. When the sun went down again and dusk fell, I watched the villagers returning from their fields, carrying bundles of firewood on their heads, driving their flocks home. I slipped through the *lantana* shrub and lay in wait by their path, well concealed behind a boulder, and pounced upon the last animal in a column, seized its throat, and made off with it. My hunger was appeased for at least two days. I could not repeat this strategy. Later when the villager realized that he had lost an animal and followed the bloodstains, I had to change my tactics, as well as my abode. I eluded the villagers again and again.

They must have begun to wonder about the shape of the predator in their midst. 'Can't be a tiger,' they must have thought, 'the hunters have taken away the entire family, by this time they'll have sold the skin of the adult, and stuffed the cubs as trophies.'

'But it was a tigress; the father must still be at large.'

'Oh, no,' the local animal expert must have explained, 'you must understand that a male tiger hardly ever lives with the family . . . Must be a visitor from another forest. Tigers are not family-bound like monkeys and other creatures. Monkeys belong to a more advanced group . . .' Human beings have their own theories, and it is always amusing to hear them talk about us. Such ignorance and self-assurance!

Presently they must have concluded: 'It could not have been a tiger at all, but a cheetah, or even a hyena, which steals up and attacks. A tiger would not be satisfied with a sheep, but always attacks larger cattle . . .'

Nowadays I chose a smaller animal from the herd, since I could manage it without leaving a trail, and eat afresh a whole thing. With a larger animal, I had to keep the kill for a second meal, and that always betrayed my presence, since it attracts the wretches who trailed me for scraps and leavings. I kept my abode constantly changing. It was safer and advantageous too to move along the mountain range. It gave me a very wide area of cover. I moved from place to place, and discovered that below the mountain range in the valleys and plains there were human habitations, to which the cattle were driven back in the evenings. I could repeat my tactics everywhere: lie in wait and seize the last one in the herd and vanish. Among those scattered villages, news spread very slowly, and that was to my advantage. I preferred my present method of seeking food – it spared me all the fatigue and uncertainty of hunting in the jungle. Jungle creatures are more alert and elusive than the village cattle, stupid creatures which could never anticipate danger even when passing under my chin while I crouched on a rock.

Village folk soon realized that they were losing their animals regularly. Some thought a devil was around, and were preparing to perform propitiatory ceremonies in their villages. Also they took care to drive their flocks back home while there was still sunlight, and had more men to guard them. This affected me adversely, but only for a short time. I began to scout around the villages at night, when the men put out the lamps and retired for the day.

Once, along a ditch running down a village street, I moved on soft foot; nothing stirred except bandicoots, scampering away. The village mongrels curled in the street dust were unaware, so silently did I move. Otherwise they would have howled and brought the entire village on me. At the centre of the village, I noticed an enclosure made of bamboo and all kinds of brambles and thorn, with a little door of the same kind. The door could not be pushed open by the stupid sheep penned within the stockade, but I could get through it without any effort. I seized the nearest creature, but before I could turn round and get out, the cry of the lamb I had caught set the whole flock bleating, crying, howling in panic, enough noise to wake up the villagers peacefully slumbering in their homes. In a moment they were out, screaming and shouting obscenities at the enemy invading their sanctum. 'Ah! Now we know! We have him. He must not escape . . .'

They came rushing down in great force holding up flaming torches, hatchets, crowbars, and staves. I was about to dash out with my prize, but in the confusion that ensued, I lost sight of the door. I had never seen humans in such a frenzy of shouting. I never knew that humans beings could be so devilish. They were all armed, aimed spears at me and hit me with arrows while I was desperately trying to find a way out. More than their weapons, the sight of their flaming torches, red-coloured and smoking viciously, was completely unnerving. I dropped the lamb, my only ambition now being to escape with my skin intact. I had never been so close to fire: sometimes in summer, we noticed forest fires far off, but they would not be frightening, and we kept our distance from them. But now the fire was choking, blinding and scorching: one fellow flung his torch at me, which singed my skin, another threw a spear which gashed my side; I ran round and round madly; I could not fall upon my pursuers as I could not see them clearly. The crowd was intent on murdering me. They were heaving huge rocks at me. Men in their frenzy seemed to have lost all fear, and boys of all ages were cursing and chasing me round and round – I could have fallen on any of them and scattered them but for the fire in their hands. It was unbearable. I was bleeding from the cuts on my face and limbs and I wished I were dead. I would have welcomed death in preference to the torture I was facing now.

Penned in the stockade, I felt hopeless and exhausted. The monsters chased and tormented me. Luckily for me a mishap occurred at this desperate moment. A boy who was capering with a torch at the end of a bamboo pole, while attempting to poke me, held his flame too close to the fence, which caught fire. Their attention was now diverted to saving the sheep. They demolished the stockade and opened a way out. Wedged between bleating sheep, which received the blows meant for me, I ran out and escaped into the night.

Looking back, I feel that I should not have chosen the easy path

– of raiding villages. Stepping into human society was a thoughtless act. Instead of living the rest of my life majestically as an honest-to-god tiger going in and out of his cave, eating and sleeping, performing no act except what he wished, Lord of the Jungle, before whom other creatures from a squirrel to a bear quaked in fear, I had let myself in for ultimate slavery. I had thought that there could never be any creature stronger than a tiger. I was mistaken. A human being may look small, without prominent teeth or claws, but he is endowed with some strange power, which can manoeuvre a tiger or an elephant as if they were toys.

After my attack on the village, people there not only began to guard their cattle better, but also approached the authorities for help. They sent their spokesmen to the town to meet the Collector and demand his help. They were vociferous and gave sensational and exaggerated reports of how a tiger was terrorizing the countryside, invading the villages and carrying away cattle, and mauling and maiming people going into the forests to gather firewood: they gave a list of names of persons who were killed. They were building a case against me and were inventing stories. I had always tried to avoid encounters with human beings, and if I had wanted, could have mangled and messed up the human creatures that had entered the stockade that night in the village. But I didn't, I didn't want to. If I had been present at that meeting with the Collector I would have proved that the villagers were lying. But I came to know of it only later in my life.

The Collector, being a man used to such representations, just said: 'I'll look into your case. I can't promise anything. How do you know that there is a tiger around?'

'We saw it.'

'How many of you saw it?'

'All of us . . .' said the deputation.

'How many persons live in your village?'

They looked at each other in consternation, being unfamiliar with numbers. 'More than a hundred, sir,' ventured an elder.

'Have all the hundred seen the tiger?' asked the Collector.

'Yes,' they chorused.

The Collector fixed his gaze on someone arbitrarily and asked, 'How big was the tiger?'

The man blinked for a minute and then indicated with his hands some size, whereupon another man pushed himself forward and said, 'He is wrong. The tiger was this big . . .'

A heated argument started, many others joined for and against, until the Collector said, 'Silence, are you both talking of the same tiger or two different ones? Was there one tiger or two or three?'

Someone said, 'Five in all, sir. Four cubs and a tigress, which were shot.'

'Who shot them?' asked the Collector.

'Some *shikari* from the town . . .'

'Which town?'

'We can't say, sir, we don't know.'

'Did they have a licence to shoot? Who gave them licence?'

The petitioners, feeling they were being dragged beyond their depths, became tongue-tied.

The Collector observed them for a moment and said, 'Have you brought your petition in writing?' They looked terrified, having no notion of the world of letters. The Collector felt compassionate and said, 'I can't take action unless there is a written petition. Go to a petition-writer . . . you'll find one in the veranda of the law court or at the market gate. Get the petition engrossed on a stamp-paper of one rupee and fifty paise, and leave it with my clerk at the office. Then I'll fix a date for inspection and take action . . . For all I know there may be no tiger whatever. You may be imagining! One mentions one tiger and another says five!' And he permitted himself a dignified grin at the joke. 'However, it is my duty to look into it, if you have a grievance.'

The deputation of villagers had to visit the Collector almost once a week, spending time and money to no purpose. From within the jungle where their villages were situated, they had to trudge ten miles to the highway and wait endlessly for a chance lift in a passing bus or lorry. At the Collector's office they could see, after much waiting, only the Collector's clerk, who took their petitions and then directed them to satisfy further official formalities. At the end of the day they returned to their villages, dreading lest the tiger should waylay them.

I had perfected my system of snatching cattle at night. I became quite familiar with their movements and timings and the weak points in the enclosures that the creatures were penned in. The villages were all alike and the villagers had similar habits in tending their sheep or cattle. They could never anticipate where I'd strike next. I covered a large perimeter. If I took a sheep from this village today, my next target would be elsewhere, in your terms, several days later. In between, they'd not know where to look for me. Some parts of Mempi hills had deep ravines, quite inaccessible to human beings. I hid myself in them and planned to attack with considerable calculation, taking care not to be seen in the same area again. I had perfected the art – no village was too far out, and no fencing was impregnable. I walked in and out of places, hardly aware at that time how very desperate the villagers were beginning to feel. They began to adopt defensive measures, such as keeping up a bonfire all night, and posting vigilant guards, armed with sharp weapons, and in one or two places they had even scattered poisoned meat for me; but I'd not touch such things – only some wildcat or mongrel nosing around ended its career then and there.

When he announced his name as Captain, they always asked, 'Of what?' He would always reply, 'Just Captain. Mister Captain, if you like.'

'Oh, we thought it was an army or football captain.' He was

used to such quips wherever he went, but he could not afford to mind it and treated it good-humouredly. A man about town, he had to be seeing people constantly on business – running his circus, which had its origin in a certain 'Grand Irish Circus'. When questioned on the Irish origin or contents of his circus, he generally explained, 'When I was down and out at Poona, I met a chap, a down-and-out Irishman, who owned a half-starved pony, a yellow monkey, and a parrot which could pick up numbers and alphabets from a stack of cards. He took them about and displayed them here and there in the city. He dispensed with his pony, selling it off to a tonga owner, and managed with the parrot and the monkey, which became his sole assets; he could maintain them inexpensively with a handful of nuts for the monkey and a guava fruit for the parrot. He had a portable signboard painted, GRAND IRISH CIRCUS, and set it up in the town hall compound, street pavements, or market square and attracted a crowd. He called himself O'Brien though he had a brown skin and never uttered a word of English or Irish but spoke only "The Native Language" in order to establish rapport with his public, as he always took the trouble to explain.' Captain always wondered what sort of an Irishman he was, but said to himself, 'If I could call myself Captain, by the same logic he could be O'Brien.' At some point in their association O'Brien took up some other business and sold his good will and the circus to Captain for fifty rupees. Captain used the signboard, monkey, and parrot to make a living following O'Brien's tradition. Feeling that he should do better, he approached one Dadhaji, owner of 'Dadhaji Grand Circus'.

The grand old man was reclining in an easy chair in his special tent. Young Captain approached him with all humility with the monkey on his shoulder and holding the parrot cage in his hand. Dadhaji watched the visitor for some time and asked, 'What do you want?'

'I want to work here, sir.'

'What do you know of animals?' Captain was afraid to give an answer. After waiting for a moment the man thundered, 'Have you no answer? Be frank. I would appreciate it. I like people young or old to be frank.'

Captain felt like turning round and fleeing. But he was standing too close to the great man to run away. His aides, standing at different points, were watching him with contempt. The only animal Captain had known was an alley cat and its mates in his boyhood in Abu Lane. And a mongrel he was fond of, which used to curl up in the street dust. The several attempts he made to shelter it in his room were frustrated by his father who was strictly anti-canine. Even after his death, Captain could not realize his ambition, since their creditors took over their property, which resulted in the scattering of the family. Captain, with his little savings in hand, set out to seek his fortune and ended up in Poona. These flashes of memory were not worth recounting, and he helplessly wished that his retreat were not blocked by all those terrible aides in grey uniform with their pockets embroidered in yellow thread: 'Dadhaji Grand Circus'. Frightening. The old man was evidently enjoying the young fellow's discomfiture. Captain felt suddenly challenged and said, 'Born and bred in Abu Lane of Malgudi town, sir, no chance, sir, of encountering animals, sir . . . The very reason why I have come to you, sir, is to learn about animals and their training.' He had found his tongue, which pleased the old gentleman.

'Ah, that's better. You should talk, otherwise you will be left out. A young chap who comes out to learn and earn must be alert. I know where we stand now. I seem to know the monkey on your shoulder and the parrot, they were once with the worthless fellow who called himself O'Connor or some such thing. Don't know where he got the idea that he was Irish – a bastard possibly out of our own slums. I am not going to waste my time asking how and where you met him and all that. It's your business. Keep that monkey, if you like, or drive it back to its treetop, so also the parrot. If you hoped that you could add them to my show, you were mistaken. They are too insignificant for my circus. When I say "show" I mean acts of large quadrupeds and bipeds, whose movements would be visible from any part of the auditorium. Otherwise it is no show. What you carry is fit for street corners; I have no use for them. Now you may go if you choose – or stay if you are willing to work here.'

Captain was fascinated by the old man's alternating moods of aggression and tenderness. 'Let me stay here, sir,' he said, 'and learn to work.'

The old man said, 'I have around one hundred and fifty animals in this camp. Are you prepared to start with the horses? You will have to clean their stables first and also groom them. And then I'll tell you what you can do. Ultimately, if you prove your worth, you will be in charge of the cages of tigers and lions. That is all for the present. You will be fed and sheltered and given pocket money. Think over this offer and give me your answer tomorrow . . .'

Captain said, 'Not tomorrow, sir. I'll stay here.'

'When I say tomorrow, I mean it. Take twenty-four hours to think it over.'

That was how Captain started his career when he was hardly twenty. Dadhaji imparted to him unreservedly all his knowledge and skill in the training of animals as well as his business methods. Dadhaji often explained his philosophy: 'There is no such thing as a wild animal – any creature on four legs can be educated if you apply the right method. For over fifty years I have lived with animals – over a hundred at a time – and I know what I am saying.'

Dadhaji began to depend on Captain more and more. When he became too old to manage things, he made him his working partner. At his death the entire circus with all its property and assets and animals were bequeathed to Captain. The transition was unnoticed since Captain had virtually been running the show for years, only presenting periodical reports to Dadhaji while he rested in his tent.

*

After Dadhaji's death, Captain shifted his circus to Malgudi. It was a mighty undertaking. He sold the ground at Poona, taking permission from the purchaser of the land to keep his animals there till he was able to move his business to Malgudi. He had enough money to negotiate for the wasteland beyond the level-crossing. Within three months the land was transformed and in big letters loomed the sign GRAND MALGUDI CIRCUS. He had originally intended to name it after the Irishman or Dadhaji, but the municipal chairman and members showed some reluctance in their attitude until he assured them that he was putting Malgudi on the world map by naming it Grand Malgudi Circus. 'Just to show my roots are here, although I must confess that I had thought of perpetuating my benefactors' names originally. Hereafter Malgudi will be the home for hundreds of animals and scores of acrobats and performers of all kinds. You will be proud of it . . .' His talk was captivating. He liberally dispensed money to smooth out the passage of all kinds of transactions and favours, and in a short while Malgudi became more famous for its circus than for its mountains and river, and Captain was viewed as the wonder man who had transformed the town.

It was the result of hard work. Captain rose at five in the morning and went on a tour of inspection. Elephants and camels and giraffes were at the eastern end of the camp. He went up there first with his chief executive Anand, who had been with him since his Poona days. He started with the camels at one end, keeping in mind Dadhaji's injunction, 'You must watch the condition of every animal and anticipate how long it will last, and get an immediate replacement if one dies. Keep an eye on the sources, if you are not to face embarrassment in public. The show never halts because of one animal.' He could judge their health and welfare by observing their stance and attitude at five in the morning. Animals, in his view, looked their brightest at that hour if they were in good health. The animals stirred and gave some indication of recognizing his presence when he approached, and that pleased him. He passed on from animal to animal, checking their welfare; if they were sick, he sent Anand to wake up the veterinarian immediately. Starting with camels, he passed on to elephants, horses and lastly to the minor performing creatures, and by the time he reached his office he would have understood the condition of every creature under his control. He sat at his desk and noted down his observations and suggestions or criticized the state of cleanliness of cages or surroundings and indicated punishments for erring assistants. When he finished his job at the table, his wife would ring the bell for breakfast.

'All our animals from the performing mongoose to the tusker are in excellent condition,' he boasted at breakfast.

'Yes,' said his wife, 'they are tended better than your family.'

'You must say something unpleasant – otherwise you are never happy.'

'Your beloved animals may also have something to say if they could speak . . .'

'What really is your grouse? I never understand. You demanded that the boys should be sent to Lovedale School; that I have done, swallowing my own ideas at such a cost!'

'Good thing too – otherwise you would have made lion-tamers of them as well.'

'I don't know why you say such things, knowing full well where the money comes from, so much needed for you and your damned family at Madras – all hangers-on, none of them will do anything except sit back and wait for my cheque every month . . . If you wish to see them get on, why don't you ask one of your brothers to come and type my correspondence at least?'

'Isn't enough that I slave for you? You want the entire "damned" family at your beck and call? I am tired of everything, my boy. As soon as you get someone to lead your trapeze team, I'll retire and go back to Madras. I'm tired of jumping and swinging and the perpetual tent-living.' When she became too trying, Captain would

[33]

abruptly leave the table. When she saw him rise, she felt uneasy and said as if nothing had happened, 'Your coffee. Want more milk, sugar?' He never answered, but just emptied the cup at one gulp and walked out of the tent. She kept looking after him and muttered, 'He has lost all sense of humour, the slightest upset and he flounces out, let him . . . I don't care. Only animals seem to be fit for his company.'

He told himself, 'Women are impossible. Worse than twenty untamed jungle creatures on one's hands at a time . . .'

Captain had gone to the Collector's office to renew some petty licence. He pricked up his ears when he heard the word 'tiger'. He was about to leave but halted his steps, remembering another of Dadhaji's injunctions. 'If you hear the word "tiger", don't leave. Stay back and find out.' And he was hearing the word 'tiger' not once but several times through the babble of four villagers. 'This is our twentieth visit and you always keep saying, "Come tomorrow" . . . Are you playing with us? You are waiting to see us and our cattle eaten by the tiger and digested before you can think of saving us.'

'Every time we have to walk from our homes ten miles for a bus to reach here,' said another.

The clerk was irritated and said, 'No one has invited you.'

'Then why did the officer promise help?'

'Ask him. Why should I answer that question?'

'Yes, if we see him. As it is, we meet only the *Pujari*, not the God in the sanctum, and the *Pujari* denies what the God promises.' And they laughed at their own quip.

'This is not his only business, he has more important work than listening to your stories.'

'Ah, stories, you think! Come and spend a night in our village and you will know.'

'My boss will inspect your village . . .'

'When? After the tiger has had his fill?'

[34]

'There is no tiger and he will not eat you,' said the clerk. 'The officer will come on inspection next month . . .'

'Next month! Next month! You have been saying it for months while the tiger is fattening himself on our cattle.'

'You get out of my office! Have you no eyes to see that I am busy now?' He beat his brow in despair. 'This is a cursed seat. No peace. I'm not allowed to clear these papers. Tomorrow when the boss comes, he will bawl his head off.' He lost his temper suddenly. 'What do you take me for? Government office is not your nuptial chamber, for you to demand things. I'll call the police if you are going to be riotous. Mind your manners. The officer will come on inspection to your village and then take necessary steps. Till then you must wait.'

Captain watched them as they left the place grumbling, but afraid to curse openly. The clerk got absorbed in his files once again, muttering, 'The officer is always on tour, what can I do if everyone comes and bothers me? Am I the officer drawing a fat salary?' This was addressed to the Captain, who was at the door, and he just said, soothingly, 'Of course, you are not,' and followed the villagers out.

He followed them a little distance, and threw out a general question in order to attract their attention, 'Are you the headman of the village?' At which they turned round and stopped.

'How did you know us, sir?'

He introduced himself. 'You see that circus there – that's mine and I often come to this office on business. Not bad fellows at this office but they delay. That poor fellow, he can't help it. Only his master has to do things . . .'

'Every time we come, we bring him some offering – cucumbers or sugar cane, pumpkin, melon, or anything. Never see him bare-handed, and yet he is unhelpful.'

Captain made himself agreeable by listening to them patiently. All that they seemed to want was a hearing. They did not know

[35]

who he was, but his dress – trousers, bush shirt and the sun-hat – impressed them, and he spoke to them in Tamil, which endeared him to them. He treated them to coloured drinks from a wayside stall, while eliciting information about the tiger. He invited them to come up and see his circus. 'I have work to do, next two days, and then I'll come to your village. If you help me I'll catch the tiger. You will have to show me where he lives.'

'We don't know, sir. We can't say. He is here, there and everywhere. We think he is a devil and has wings and not an ordinary creature. We saw him only once ... We would have burnt him with the torches and cooked him alive but he escaped. He slips in and out, and can never be caught or killed ... He is no ordinary creature. Before we can notice, he snatches away even the biggest buffalo, and vanishes.'

'He is an ordinary tiger, black and yellow, with four legs and only one tail and no extraordinary creature. I'll deal with him, don't worry. I'll see you on Thursday next ...'

He took directions from them to reach the village, and was with them on the appointed day. The village was set far into the jungle, a single street and about thirty homes of bricks or just thatched huts, and a lot of cattle and sheep – mostly a pastoral community. He had gone in a small car, but he had to leave it on the main highway and walk down to the village, which was full of excitement. Women and children stood around him. Most of the men were out working in the fields. Seeing Captain's grey uniform, the boys cried, 'The police have come,' and ran around to fetch the men, who recognized him and cried, 'Oh, it's our hunter, who is going to kill the tiger.'

Captain corrected them. 'I'm not going to kill, but take him away ...' Some rushed into their homes and brought out ancient stools and benches and offered him seats. Some brought him tender coconut and chipped off the top and offered him a drink. Others brought him papaya and banana. Captain felt overwhelmed by their hospitality and promised, 'I will see that you are not bothered by the tiger. But you must all help me. I must know where he is and how he comes and goes and where he keeps himself during the day.'

'Oh, that's difficult, sir. If we follow him, he may turn round and attack.'

'If you don't tell me where the tiger is, how can I catch him? I may also begin to think, like those officials, that you are all fancying the tiger.'

At this they protested. 'Even two days ago, two fellows who were out to cut wood were mutilated – one fellow lost an arm.'

'Will you take me to him?'

'Not in our village, but there on the other side of the hillock . . .'

'Will you come with me and show me the man and where he was attacked, so that I may find out the tiger's movements?' Strangely they seemed to be averse to this procedure. The victims of the tiger seemed as elusive as the tiger itself. They would complain and pour forth their grievances, but somehow at the same time show reluctance to help him directly. They would not be explicit about the attacks. But Captain would not give up. He changed his tactics. He contacted the forest guards, offered a fee for information about the tiger, followed their tips. Leaving much of his circus work to his chief executive, he unrelentingly pursued the tiger, and finally arrived at the rivulet beyond which was the cave at the tail end of the Mempi range. Captain had taken special precautions to camouflage himself with certain types of foliage. He hoisted himself onto the branch of a tree and stayed there all night in the company of the forest guards, and finally had a glimpse of the tiger returning to his cave.

Although I was cautious and avoided all the traps laid for me, ultimately I yielded to a temptation, and that proved to be the end. After trying many hideouts, I had come back to my original home.

[37]

As I emerged from my lair late one evening, passing through the long grass, I heard a bleating and, following the sound, saw a well-fed goat in front of me. I hesitated only for a moment, looked about, took a leap and landed on its back. At the same time I heard a strange, unfamiliar clattering noise – an iron door came down and shut me in. I was trapped. I was at once surrounded by unfamiliar figures and heard strange voices. A flashlight was pointed at me and a man was saying, 'Just what I was looking for. A magnificent fellow."

'Mr Captain, isn't he rather big for our purpose?'

'No, he is just right. Only we may have to starve him for a while.'

'Will you be able to make him obedient?'

'Of course,' said the other. 'You will see, I'll make him a star.'

'It seems to me he is too heavy for our purpose.'

'He is all right. He'll become slim and agile. Leave it to me.' Then he turned round and said to someone, 'Pay off all the men who have helped us in trapping. Give them an extra tip, but make sure that their services are terminated. Keep the six men from our own staff, and they will take care of the business of wheeling this cage to the town. It may take four days, if drawn by bullocks. All along the way crowds will watch and follow; that will be an excellent advertisement for our circus.'

My Master, later in my life, has mentioned hell, describing the conditions that would give one a feel of it. Now, recollecting the day of my trapping and the journey onward, I realize its meaning. The trap was narrow and I felt cribbed and cramped. I, who had lived a full and free life – stretching myself as I pleased, or burying myself in the jungle grass – now had to keep standing as the trap on wheels was drawn along. A pair of bullocks was yoked to it and the driver kept yelling and whipping them; the wheels rolled on rough ground, and I was jolted from side to side. I felt strangely uncomfortable to be moving without the use of my legs! First time experiencing locomotion. They had screened the trap with a lot of foliage, so that I might not see the bullocks or the driver; they had some irrational fear that if I saw them, I might want to eat them up. They forgot that the goat which was the bait was still in my company – although not alive.

Through many villages and towns they took me. My captors walked along behind the cage. Now and then they stopped under a wayside tree and unyoked the bullocks to give them rest. At such times the front portion of the carriage rested on the ground, and the floor sloped forward and I kept sliding down, with the remains of the goat flowing over me. It was uncomfortable, and I had to roar out my displeasure. The noise I made scared the spectators surrounding my cage and sent them running. My guards broke into laughter and shouted at the crowd, 'If you are so scared of the tiger locked up in the cage, what'll you do if we open the door and let it out?' This was their way of joking. And then much talk, inevitable wherever human beings are gathered. For one used to the grand silence of the jungle, the noisy nature of humanity was distressing. In due course, I got used to it. When I imbibed my Master's lessons, I realized that deep within I was not different from human beings, and I got into their habit myself and never had a moment's silence or stillness of mind – I was either talking (in my own way, inaudibly) or listening, and thus became fully qualified to enter human society.

After days, how many I didn't know and could not reckon, we came to a stop. The sides of the cage were still screened with brambles and foliage and I had no idea where we were. I only heard, as usual, a lot of talk and shouting and counter-shouting, and much movement outside. Suddenly all the twigs and foliage screening the cage were torn away and I saw through the bars a new world such as I could never have imagined in my life – a stretch of land with no trees or rocks or long grass or bamboo clusters or *lantana* bushes or other undergrowth, but bare and clean ground as far as I could see, ending in what I learnt was a big tent surrounded by smaller tents and shacks, the whole ground swarming with bipeds. I had no notion that the earth contained so many human creatures. Naturally they stared and gaped and talked. I tried to head my way out by pushing, and hurt myself in the attempt.

Now I saw a man with a long staff in hand standing close by, saying, 'Want to get out? All right, come on . . .' and he poked with the staff and laughed when I protested. 'Ah, what a beautiful voice. If you were a singer, you could enchant an audience of thousands without a mike,' and laughed at his own joke. Others laughed with him too. I learnt later that they were obliged to laugh at his jokes, being his subordinates. As I went along I learnt that he was the owner of the circus. He was the one who met me when I was trapped, and he was to be my commander for years to come. He now poked the staff through the bars and was greatly amused when I jumped about in pain and confusion. He said with a guffaw, 'Ah, you are a promising dancer too!' He turned to his assistant and said, 'Let us advertise – a tiger *Bharatnatyam*, something that no circus has ever attempted.'

'Yes, sir, that's an excellent idea, sir,' said Captain's 'yes-man' who was always by his side agreeing with everything he said, his second-in-command.

'We will teach this fellow every accomplishment in due course,' said Captain. 'But our immediate job is to drive him into the other cage, which is going to be his new home.' He prodded me with his staff and hit me to the accompaniment of stentorian commands; I was to hear the voice again and again in the years to come. Also he drew the staff along the cage's bars, creating a rat-tat noise which confused me. When I tried to understand what it meant, he withdrew the staff and jabbed my side with it. I was miserable and did not know where to keep myself. He gave me no rest, but drove me round and round with that staff in the narrow space till in sheer

[40]

desperation, edging away from the probing stick, I dashed on and found myself in another cage, where the door immediately came down. This was my first act of obedience. Captain now withdrew his staff and said, 'Ah, good. Stay there.' He said to his yes-man, 'Take the other cage for cleaning – awful mess, stinks to the high heavens.'

As night fell, I could see more clearly. I heard a lion roar, and the voices of other jungle fellows; and over all that, of course, human talk in different keys. I saw only empty grounds before me and a glow of lights somewhere. I was bewildered and did not know why I was brought here, or what they were planning to do with me. Captain and his yes-man would come off and on, stand looking at me, say something between themselves, and then leave. It was irksome to stay in that cramped space all day and night – my only activity being lying down and getting up, and again lying down and getting up, stretching myself to the extent possible, and turning round and round, grumbling and whining. But no one cared. Being used to the vastness and freedom of jungle life, I found this an impossible condition of living. I could do nothing more than pace up and down in despair.

For three days I did not feel hungry. On the fourth day I felt a stab of hunger and did not know what to do about it: how was my hunger going to be appeased? This was hell, as defined by my Master, an endless state of torment with no promise of relief or escape. I still had no conception that food could come one's way without a chase. These were the stages of knowing attained through suffering. I can hardly describe that kind of suffering, an emptiness, a helplessness, and a hopelessness behind the bars. Now, of course, I have got used to it, after years of circus life and then the zoo. But at that time I just had no conception of that kind of life. Bars of iron, unbending and perpetually pressing against one's face. I had had no contact with any sort of metal in my life; now this combination of man and metal subdued me – metal which in various forms served the evil ends of man as prison bars, traps, and weapons. I desperately tried to smash the bars again and again and only made my head bloody. When Captain viewed me in this state, he only laughed and remarked to his aide, 'All these stupid creatures are alike! They all expect the bars of the cage to be made of butter. No harm if he learns the facts of life in his own way!' And they left me alone.

I began to despair when they left. When Captain showed himself outside my cage, a hope always rose in me, however slight, that some improvement was likely in my lot. That was probably the way he worked, driving me on to look on him ultimately as my Saviour. He was considered to be an expert in animal training and deeply versed in their psychology. I began to look forward to his company. Pacing around that cage, I'd pause to press my nose close to the bars to watch the direction of his coming. He'd look at me and ask, 'How are you, sir? Learn to be a good boy and I'll make you happy . . .' I had no idea how to become a good boy and attain happiness. He continued to make me suffer loneliness, immobility, and above all hunger. For the last, I was hoping that he'd let me out now and then to hunt for food. He didn't seem to think that way.

Later, when I explained this stage of my life to my Master, he said, 'You probably in a previous life enjoyed putting your fellow-beings behind bars. One has to face the reaction of every act, if not in the same life, at least in another life or series of lives. There can be no escape from it. Now you have a chance to realize how your prisoners must have felt in those days, when you locked them in and watched them day by day to measure how far you had succeeded in breaking their spirits.'

'Why should I have done that?'

'I can't answer it; people only follow their inclinations, and sooner or later find their reward or retribution. That's the natural law of life, as inevitable as the ripening of a mango in its season or the fall of a withered leaf.'

For days they kept me without food and water. Only Captain with his companion would come to observe me, and then comment, and leave. I lost all my strength and could hardly stand up, much less pace around my cage. Even that little movement was lost; I might be a carcass for all it mattered. In this state my cage was moved one day and the door opened. I was let into a larger enclosure. I jumped out gratefully, but I found that my legs could not support me. But Captain was there at the centre of the enclosure and would not let me lie down. He was uttering a command in a voice which could be audible in the next jungle. He held a long whip in one hand and a chair in the other. He lashed my face several times. My face smarted. I had never experienced such pain before. When I tried to ward off his attack, he wielded the chair as a shield. With my paws I could only hit the chair, and he constantly poked my face with it. He commanded, 'Run, run,' and kept repeating it with every lashing.

To my shame and dismay, this was being watched by other animals, beyond the enclosure. First time I was setting eyes on those odd, unfamiliar creatures. I could not understand what species they belonged to. Some of them were tethered to a post, some were free, some in different types of cages. Among the birds I could recognize a parrot, but not some of the long-legged ones. A grotesque one was the camel. I was aghast at its height and humps. A majestic animal, to my surprise a grass-eater, I was told was a horse – there were many of them; a meaner version of the horse, not so handsome either, was also there, a donkey. Another one that took my breath away was a hippopotamus, which I mistook for a piece of ill-shaped mountain. Of course I could recognize the ape, which moved about freely – shaggy one with awkward swinging arms, which seemed to be well integrated in human society, able to move with humans on equal terms . . . I had a glimpse of a bear, but no deer, which did not seem to have come to the notice of Captain. So far so good for them; only cursed creatures, weighed down with the *karma* of their previous lives, seemed to have come to his notice, who wielded his chair and whip like a maniac. I now understand that he had held me up as a lesson to other creatures, of what awaited them if they did not obey. At least they were fortunate in knowing how to show their obedience. They were all excellent performers; I was to become a colleague of theirs.

I was ignorant, bewildered, and in pain. It'd have been a relief to be able to pounce on that man and leave it to chance for one of us to survive. But that chair which he held made it impossible for me to approach him, while his whip could reach me all over. He was crying out like a frenzied creature, 'Run, run, come on!' While I stood paralysed and in great suffering, I heard one of those watching animals suggest to me in our language, which no tyrant could suspect or suppress as it would sound like merely a grunt or a sigh, 'He wants you to run round and round as if stung by bees at your backside. Do it and he will stop beating you. Otherwise you have no chance.' I couldn't guess where the message came from – could be the elephant placidly munching sugar cane, giving no suspicion of ever noticing my predicament, except through a corner of his eye. Ah, that was a great help.

I said to my well-wisher, 'But I feel faint, can't stand on my feet, starving, not even a drink of water.'

'Never mind. You will get everything – only run round as he commands. He is a madcap and we must learn to live with him. We are in his hands.'

'Why do you tolerate him? Any one of us can stamp him out.'

'Not so easily, he is really stronger than ten of us. Once all of us tried and were sorry for it . . .' Mutual communication was one privilege left for us animals: human beings could not interfere with our freedom of speech because they never suspect that we have our own codes, signals, and idioms. Fortunately they usually did not notice when we grunted, hissed or sighed, but when they did, they would talk among themselves anxiously: 'Poor thing is making peculiar noises, I hope it is not going to be sick. Must tell the veterinarian to look over the beast: it must be in perfect form for the show tomorrow, for the specially advertised item, otherwise the public will smash the chairs and the gallery . . .'

The ape was the most light-hearted of all. He was the happiest animal in the circus, walking about freely in human company, fondly clinging to the finger of one or the other – even holding hands with Captain sometimes. He must be conceited, fancying himself to be a human being; smoking cigarettes, sitting in chairs and drinking tea from cups, wearing trousers and coat and cap and spectacles, and chattering merrily all the time. His acts in the ring were not different from what he did outside the ring – except a cycle ride combined with trapeze acts. He continuously chattered, grinned and grimaced – a happy soul. In my first glimpse of him, he also added a word of his own: 'Hey tiger, run round and round as our boss demands. Let us hope and pray we'll see the day when he'll do the running and we shall hold the whip . . . Anyway, till that good day arrives, obey him and that simpleton will protect and feed us – we are at least spared the trouble of seeking food and preserving ourselves from enemies. He is doing all that for us. He is a damned fool, but doesn't know it; thinks that he is the Lord of the Universe.'

'At one time, I had also thought so of myself,' I said.

I ran round and round in circles in pursuit of nothing – and that seemed a very foolish senseless act. At least a hare running ahead would have provided a show of reason for running. But that's how Captain seemed to want it; I held my breath, and though my eyes were darkening with faintness, I ran and kept running as long as he kept the whip cracking in the air without touching my back – and that was some improvement indeed. He went gyrating round and round following my movement. It seemed as much hard work for him as for me. When the cracking of his whip ceased, I too stopped. It was not possible to run any more. I was ready to fall into a faint and probably breathe my last; breath coming and going so fast. When I came near my cage I found the door open and leaped in and lay down – expecting to be killed outright for my disobedience. But when I opened my eyes, I saw Captain outside looking at me more kindly than ever. 'Well, that was a fine performance. I now have confidence that we can use him.' The whip and the chair were put away and he was unarmed, and that itself seemed to me a good sign. My cage was wheeled away to its original place, away from other animals. I was sorry because I felt better watching others and being in communion with them. Just as I was closing my eyes, some warders poled and prodded me to move to another cage. I was happy to find there pieces of meat and a trough of water. My first piece of education.

I understood the business now and the routine to be followed. Every day at the same hour they would drive me into a wheeled cage and draw it to the larger enclosure and let me out, where Captain waited with chair and whip. The moment the door was raised and the whip was flourished, I started running round and round. Then back to the cage, to be wheeled off to my home, which I found cleaned and washed and with food kept for me. That was very welcome. I'd have nothing more to do for the rest of the day. Life was not so bad after all. Captain was not such a monster after all. I began to respect him for his capabilities. I began to admire him – a sort of worshipful attitude was developing in me. I had thought in the jungle that I was supreme. Now that was gone. I was a defeated king, and Captain was the unquestioned suzerain. After all, what he expected of me seemed so simple – instead of understanding it, I allowed myself to be beaten, and suffered through ignorance. And running around the enclosure was quite beneficial for one cooped up in a cage all day.

But soon I was to realize that that was not all. It was only a preparation. When I became an adept at running, I was ready for the next stage of education. The more difficult part was still to come.

I was let out into the enclosure as usual one day, Captain alert as ever with his chair and whip. At the crack of the whip, I started running as usual, but I found my passage obstructed by a strange object which I later knew as a stand, placed across my path. I checked my pace, at which he let out a cry, 'Jump! Go on, jump!' and the whip came lashing on me. All the good name I had earned and the good feeling I had developed for Captain seemed to be lost. I felt infuriated at the lashing and felt like jumping on him; but he held that terrible chair. Now I know a chair is a worthless, harmless piece of furniture but at that time I dreaded the sight of it. It appeared to me a mighty engine of destruction. How Captain and men like him could ever have realized how a chair would look to a tiger is really a wonder. Now I have enough understanding of life to smash a chair if it is flourished before my eyes. But then a chair looked terrible. When I was lashed, once again all the old terror of not knowing what I should do came back to me. My friends who had advised me on the first day were not there. They had been taken away to some other part of the camp by their trainers; it was a vast world where many activities took place according to Captain's plans.

I stumbled on the obstacle and kicked it away and ran on my usual round. This enraged Captain, and he came dashing behind me shouting in a frenzy, 'Jump! Jump!' and applying the whip liberally. I thought that this man was unsteady, alternating between occasional sanity and general madness. At the moment he was in the latter phase. What did he mean by bothering me like this, forcing me to do some obscure act? I ran hither and thither and tried to run back into the cage. That made him more angry. He came after me in a delirium and hit me as I crouched trembling in the cage. He shouted and ordered me out; I jumped out and started running round and came against the hurdle once again, knocked it down and ran hither and thither and went back into the cage. Red in the face and panting like an engine, Captain ordered, 'Take the devil away. Off rations for three days, not even water, and he will come round, you will see . . .' He kept glaring at me.

Now I follow human speech, by the grace of my Master, but in those days I was dense and did not know what the word 'jump' meant, and suffered untold misery. Today I would have immediately understood that Captain wished me to cross the hurdle in a jump and proceed to go round, come back to the hurdle and jump over it again and again until he was satisfied that I had mastered the art. Absolutely a pointless accomplishment, but Captain had set his heart on it. On the day I understood and performed it, he was beside himself with joy. He stroked my back with the whip handle as I gratefully rushed back to my cage and said, 'Good. Keep it up; now you have earned your dinner . . .'

Every day I was put through this exercise. After a course of this, the next was only an elaboration of it. A few more obstacles were placed along the course of my run and they had to be cleared with the same smartness. My only aim now was to please Captain, and when I did that I got the reward, pieces of meat and water and undisturbed sleep in my cage. The hurdles were of different kinds, some labyrinth-like, some so twisted that I feared I might get permanently crooked. Into some I had to crawl on my belly and then out; some hurdles would lead me back to my starting point, and I had to clear them at the same speed, while he went gyrating like a spring doll, cracking his whip and commanding: 'Come on, come on, don't waste your time.' He held a watch in his hand and timed my run and movements, so that whatever perverse design he might have, I had to come through to the starting point at the same time. During the actual performance, he would announce: 'Raja is now running at a speed of sixty miles an hour, the pace he generally maintains while chasing game in the jungle. From his starting point in the ring back to the same spot in two minutes five seconds. Whether he goes one round or several rounds he will maintain the same speed. After that you will see him go through several kinds of obstacles, hurdles and mazes . . . You will see, ladies and gentlemen, that whatever the hurdle, he clears it and finishes his round within the same time, adjusting his pace appropriately. He is uncanny in his timing. Anyone who wants to prove that he takes more time and I am wrong, is welcome to step in here and hold this stop-watch I have in hand. Anyone who can prove that he takes even one more second than what I have claimed will get a reward of five hundred rupees . . .' And he flourished five fresh one-hundred-rupee notes in the air. Quite a few in the audience came down but, finding that they were expected to stand within the enclosure to try their luck, withdrew.

Captain had a vast army working for him – trapeze artistes, clowns, trainers of monkeys and parrots and so on, horse riders, elephant and camel men. Each one handled a particular animal and had influence over it; there was one who could even make the hippo climb some height and occupy a stool. Every one of them had his peculiarities and problems and had to be kept in good humour as well as discipline. Captain's wife, Rita, was at the head of the trapeze team. He had many workers, who pulled, pushed, unrolled carpets and set up fences, furniture, and various other properties, and changed them quickly for the next item. As I became an established member of that circus, I was not isolated any more, but was allowed to stay around Captain in my cage. Thus I was able to watch him all day. And I also picked up a lot of information from other gossiping animals when we were kept near each other. The chimp was always bursting with news. Whenever we gathered together our main topic was the boss. He had other animals including a lion, which remained aloof but kept roaring incessantly, stimulating all other animals to make a noise. When Captain wanted quiet, he would go round cracking his whip and shout 'Shut up!' in a thundering voice, overwhelming the lion's roar. At that time, I only knew that he had some concern for me, but I was not ripe enough to grasp the meaning of what was happening. Only in recollection now can I appreciate Captain's energy and power and the variety of tasks he was able to perform: to be successful and provide all that variety and quantity of food for us, also appear on stage, and do a great deal of off-stage work too, such as checking accounts, making payments, handling his men and so forth, activities that would go on far into the night. In the midst of all this he would also be thinking of new turns and tricks and novelties to announce to the public.

He called his a Creative Circus. After getting an idea he would shut himself in his tent, do some paper work, call up his chief executive, and say, 'Here is a new idea, see how it can be worked out.' It was not his habit to consult but only to issue orders. He would just state what he wanted done and then tell his staff to achieve it in practical terms. They were not to say yes or no but only proceed with it. Now Captain called his chief executive and said, 'It's time to give a new twist to the trapeze items. It will be a sensation if the trapeze act also includes two somersaults in the air and then a passage through a ring of fire – I've thought out the details to some extent. I realize that a fireproof undervest for the artistes, which doesn't show, will be the first requisite . . . Here's a sketch I have made of the position of the ring in relation to the swings and the net below – you work out the mechanical details and modalities. Bring your report tomorrow morning.'

The executive came up next day with the report, after working on it all night, but said, 'Madam is not for any change.' Captain brooded over it for a moment and said, 'Put Lyla in Madam's place . . . the rehearsals must begin soon.' Lyla was number two in the team.

This issue precipitated a domestic crisis. That night much shouting could be heard in their home tent. Madam threatened to quit the show once and for all. She said, 'I'm not prepared to spare any of my girls or set fire to myself just to please your fancy. I'm not an orthodox wife preparing for *sati*.'

He retorted, 'Look, don't talk like that. I'm not planning to set fire to you, you know that; I'm only thinking how we could give the public something new, some new thrills. Public must find it rather stale to see you and your girls in your satin tights swing up and down.'

Here his speech was cut short by the lady saying, 'You think our items are cheap and that easy? Have you any idea how every second one's life is being risked? You think whipping and bullying dumb beasts the only great act? Why don't you come up on the swing at least once and try, instead of talking theories?'

'You forget, my dear, that I did trapeze at one time, that's how I started, but I outgrew it . . .'

'Naturally, you had to give it up, otherwise the swings might have snapped or the roof itself might have come down.'

'Since you fancy your figure has remained unchanged, I am suggesting you try and put it to some use so as to make people say "This lady is capable of more than jumps and twists in the air, she can pass through fire rings so easily, being slim!" '

'Why don't you put your head down your lion's throat and sing a popular song?'

'You are not suggesting anything original . . . I'm planning it, maybe for the Jubilee Show.'

'You are constantly talking of Jubilee. What sort of a Jubilee are you celebrating? May I know?' she asked cynically.

He ignored her remark and continued, 'If you are not interested in the new trapeze act, keep off, that's all. The show will go on . . .'

Such a determined man that he planned, prepared, rehearsed this fiery act and presented it to the public later at what he called the

Jubilee Show. Rita went through the act, unwilling to let Lyla take her place. The accuracy and timing with which the artistes performed their trapeze acts, somersaulted and shot through a flaming ring before coming to rest on the safety net below, was exciting and repeatedly applauded by the audience. But this happened at a later phase of my story. Let me go back to my training period.

After I had become an adept in racing over and through a variety of obstacles, I expected to be left alone. I was ignorant of the fact that it was only a preparation for another stage. What Captain had in mind could not be guessed by anyone. He always allowed an interval between stages of training so that I'd live in an illusion of having nothing more to do. But just as I was resting, my cage would be drawn to the training enclosure and there I'd find Captain waiting, whip in hand. When I saw him thus, I would wish we could talk it over and come to an understanding instead of going through the hard way to get a pat on my back for understanding his wishes.

Today he held a new terror for me. It was not enough that I ran around fast and also through the hurdles. At one point, while rounding a bend, I saw fire and shrank back. I thought, 'Kill me now, but I won't go near the fire.' I was reminded of the village fire when flaming torches nearly roasted me. I shrank back and naturally the whip came down and bruised me more than ever. He would not allow me to retreat from the fire, nor go round it or away from it. He blocked all my movement with his person, shielded only with the chair, while his whip could reach me from quite a distance: the state I was in, I could have easily destroyed him without a trace. Driven by desperation, panic and fury, I had to content myself with roaring out, 'Leave me alone, you monster.' But he overshouted me: 'Raja, come on through that ring, in there, come on, come on . . .' The uproar and pandemonium we both created must have been heard all over the town. I snarled, showed my teeth, wrinkled my nose, opened my mouth and shut it, and growled as if the earth were rumbling. But he was unaffected and warded me off with his chair, and pushed me closer and closer to that fire. All my movement was restricted in such a way as to leave no room for me to move or turn except through the fire. First time my belly was singed but in course of time I could pass without touching the flames. And when I performed diligently I became Captain's favourite again; with meat and water back in my cage, I was once again left to laze and live in the delusion that my trials had ended and I was going to live a happy and free life hereafter.

The next piece of training was surprisingly mild. I was driven on round and round and then stopped where a stool had been placed. I had to sit on it dangling my tail on the floor. A saucer of milk was placed on a table. I was again and again forced to sit up in front of the saucer with Captain howling 'Drink, drink, drink!' and holding his chair up; he bent down and put out his tongue over the saucer to indicate what I was expected to do. I watched completely baffled, but he was untiring in imitating the act of drinking off a saucer. 'Lower, lower,' he was howling. 'Put head down and tongue out, tongue out,' and he cracked the whip. When he did that I knew that the next would be on my back. I was quite desperate to understand him. Surely he was not expecting me to drink that white stuff in the saucer. It looked like poison to me. But there was no escape from it. He hit me so hard while I had my head down that I had to bend further down with my tongue out. No sooner had my tongue touched the saucer than I was seized with nausea and a fit of sneezing. What stuff was it, tasting so awful?

Later that day the chimp strolled along near my cage. How I envied his freedom! I wished I could also go about like him. But a tiger seemed to have a curse on it – no one can tolerate the sight of a tiger walking freely about, being burdened with size, might, and the fierce make-up that nature has given us. What a blessing to be the stature of an ape! Human beings approve of him because he approximates to their idea of what a creature should be in appearance and size. The ape was grinning as he clutched the bars of my cage and asked, 'How did you like it?'

'What?' I asked.

'The milk in the saucer which you had to lick up.'

'Terrible,' I said. 'Why should I drink it?'

'You will see for yourself soon. Why, don't you like it?'

'How can anyone like that terrible stuff?'

'Human kids are brought up on it right from birth. Men think no end of it.'

'Do you drink it?'

'Yes, of course, I don't mind it, but I prefer banana and what they aptly call monkey-nuts.'

'Why do you have to drink it?'

'Can't help it, when Captain thinks it is good for us, we have to take it.'

'What is it made of?'

He answered, 'It is made by the cow inside, and is squeezed out by men every day.'

'Every day? But don't they have to kill it to get it?'

'It is drawn out without killing the cow – so that they are able to have it every day.'

It seemed to me a strange world into which I was drawn. I said, 'It is evil tasting. Surprising it should be found in the cow, which itself tastes so good. I won't drink that stuff whatever may happen!' Before I could ask for further explanations he hopped down and was off.

By the time I could get a pat of approval on my back from Captain, I had become resigned to the taste of milk. After that a new item cropped up. As I looked up from the saucer at a training session, I found seated opposite me across the table a goat – an extraordinary thing to happen. I thought I was being specially rewarded with fresh food for accepting the milk, though it made my head reel . . . A goat sitting up with a tiger as an equal – what a crazy situation! No goat would ever dare do such a thing. Anyway I'd accept the gift and get the milk taste out of my tongue. I gave a shout of joy and the usual victory cry before pouncing across the table. But when I stirred, I was whipped back to my seat and the goat was withdrawn. When I was back in my seat, another pan of milk appeared and the goat was back in his seat. I could not understand. This kind of jugglery was disturbing. Sitting on my haunches was irksome and painful: the sight of the pan of milk was offensive and the goat was appetizing. But what was happening was beyond my understanding. What perversity that I should consume what I hated and leave what I would relish! There seemed to be an eerie indestructibility about the goat and the pan of milk. Any other goat would have run away or vanished into my belly. This sort of dodging and reappearing – I didn't like it. It was confusing, maddening, I didn't like it at all. I went at it again and again, and it disappeared and reappeared after I had been whipped back to my seat. Ultimately I realized that it'd be best to keep still, and take no notice of the goat. If it was not meant for me, why were they offering it? The ways of Captain were mysterious. Whatever he had in mind, he seemed to be able to express it only through violence. How I wished that he could speak my language or I his. There was no meeting ground beween us, but still we had so much to do with each other all the time. That was the irony of fate. Captain was convinced that if he bellowed deafeningly I'd understand, stupid fellow; although I had to admire him for several reasons.

Ultimately by sheer doggedness he made me realize that I was to ignore the goat. If I had realized it was only a dummy for purposes of practice, it'd have been quite simple. But it was so lifelike, I was deceived. I ignored it now. I sat peacefully, hoping as usual that my trial was ended and that I could go back to my home. But there could be no such thing as the end in my life. The end of one trouble was but the beginning of another. Here I was disciplined enough not to move a muscle in the presence of that supposed goat. I do not know at what point they had substituted the real one. But it bleated and that roused me. I involuntarily tensed, but Captain was too watchful and shouted, 'Stay back, Raja,' and that was enough warning for me. The stupid goat forgot its perils and became greedy at the sight of the milk; it immediately put its head down and lapped the saucer dry, and sat up to look at me as if to ask, 'What next?' Captain directed it with the slightest flourish of his whip and without any display of the chair. He looked pleased at the performance of the goat. With a smile on his face, he ordered for more milk, just as I was feeling relieved that the terrible drink was gone.

When another supply of milk came, he said, 'Raja, now that milk is for you. Lower your head and drink that milk.' What an impossible torture! I'd have preferred to have that goat sitting and blinking before me. I couldn't understand what he kept it for. Milk indeed! I hesitated, noticed a slight movement of the whip and bent down to the saucer, pretended to lick the milk, and sat back, as well as I could. Next it was the goat's turn. Captain ordered it with a slight wave of the whip, and the goat bent down and licked the plate dry. It was surprising how much milk that goat could consume. It looked as if it were Captain's intention to fill the goat to bursting point. He filled up the saucer again and again. It was merciful of him not to order me to drink the whole lot each time; he was satisfied if I dampened my nose or tongue, and then I could resume my seat. This went on all afternoon. The goat finished his portion first and then whatever remained in the plate after my show of drinking. Though I had by this time been forced to get used to the proximity of the goat, I began to hope that the goat might explode loudly with the quantities of the milk inside him and when that happened they would surely pass him on to me as they would have no further use for him. We had to be licking the milk alternately that whole day. I felt completely exhausted when I was allowed to return to my cage, and could hardly eat when my meat was brought in because of the lingering smell of milk. I just sank down and slept.

Next day I was put through a new set of exercises. I had to sit still until the goat had started lapping it up and then take my mouth to the saucer at the same time and pretend to enjoy the drink in his company. This was a trying moment as the proximity of the goat's head and its flavour was overpowering. I was perplexed at the way the whole thing was working out. I was amazed at the foolhardiness of the goat, which enjoyed its milk notwithstanding possible annihilation any moment. We had to rehearse this piece day by day until I was supposed to cultivate a taste for milk and an apparent distaste for the goat. When Captain was satisfied with the results, he made me rehearse the whole series, starting with running round through obstacles and fire, and coming to rest for a saucer of milk. (He set special value on this part and announced it with fanfare for the Jubilee Show, where it was to be presented as a Four-in-One Act.) Before the Jubilee he presented me in single-item acts, each once a week. He announced me to the public as 'that miracle tiger Raja – the magnificent'. I must have indeed looked grand and mighty with my yellow and black acquiring a special gloss, possibly through doses of milk imbibed each day. He explained that I was not an ordinary, commonplace tiger but an intelligent creature, almost human in understanding. (He was prophetic.) 'He can read the time . . .' He always held up his stop-watch in my face before I started my round of runs, saying, 'Mark the time, Raja, and keep up your speed.'

Captain presented his shows six months in a year in Malgudi town. A team of men went round to the villages in the district clad in fancy costumes and with the beat of drums and a megaphone advertised the circus. They drove around village streets in a Model T Ford painted black and yellow to remind one of the tiger. They

[57]

went up to Kommal, the farthest village, nearly fifty kilometres from Malgudi. On festivals and holidays the patrons arrived by bus, lorry, bullock-carts, and bicycles for the show; coming into the town for the circus was an exciting event for villagers, who turned up in family groups and camped in the town under the shade of trees, in the veranda of Albert Mission College, or in their wagons after unyoking the bullocks and leaving them to graze in the fields. At every show all seats in the galleries were taken as were the benches and wooden chairs and the squatting space on bare ground not far from the stage. Six cushioned seats were always kept in reserve for a hierarchy of local officials on whose goodwill depended Captain's survival.

When the monsoon set in, in October-November, the circus moved out of Malgudi to other centres in a long caravan, parading the animals, which made the circus known all along the way; the central office at Malgudi worked all through the year.

At every show, Captain made a speech, sometimes autobiographical and sometimes to boost a special act, such as mine. He delivered his message in at least three languages, as he explained: '. . . in Hindi since it is our national language and given to us by Mahatma Gandhi himself; also in English because as our beloved respected leader Nehru put it, it opens a window on the world. In Tamil, because it is, ah, our Mother Tongue, in which our greatest poets like Kamban and Valluvar composed; also the sublime inspiring patriotic songs of Bharathi, who can ever forget them?' Whatever the language, he spoke flamboyantly, always touching upon his personal life. 'Ladies and gentlemen, friends, Romans, and countrymen, as Shakespeare said, I love my circus and the animals that have made my business a success; and I have pitched my tent here because I love Malgudi; I love Malgudi because I was born and grew up here. I was a backwoods boy – living and playing in the dust of Abu Lane. They sent me, hoping to make a scholar of me, to Albert Mission School, but fate willed it otherwise.

I won't waste your time recounting my adventures while you are all eager to see the performance begin. You will see my life history in book form (a shiny colourful brochure with his portrait on the cover) sold at the gate at cost price, so that young people may cultivate ambition and a spirit of adventure and bring our nation a great name . . . All that I wish to say is that the great circus master Dadhaji of Poona adopted me and trained me though I looked like a vagrant and was indeed one; and he employed me at first to clean the stables and then taught me how to educate animals. I cannot begin the show without bowing in homage and gratitude to the memory of that great master . . .'

Captain was considerate and helped us conserve our energies by regulating our rest periods. On off days he sent away all the herbivores to forage in the lower reaches of Mempi range – camels, horses, elephants, and zebra went out in a sort of parade through the streets of Malgudi and returned in time for the next show. A set of animals always had at least two days' rest between performances. He did a lot of paperwork beforehand, scheduling each animal's duty and off-hours in a month. He studied the roster containing the names of animals (he had christened every one of the animals in his collection) and drew up a sort of chart for each one of them. The most strenuous part of their lives was during the training period. At that stage he was unsparing; and if they perished during the training, he took it as an inevitable risk of his trade. Once they were trained to perform, he viewed them as his assets to be protected, his own prosperity depending on their welfare.

He bestowed special attention to my part of the work. It always came after the trapeze sequence, which was his wife's show. He never made any speech for introducing her – a matter which made her grumble from time to time. But he just waved her off: 'Everyone knows what a grand team you lead, your girls are famous and need no introduction, also it'd sound odd to boost one's wife.'

'While your wit and eloquence are reserved only for the tiger and the rest, I suppose.'

'Yes, they need introduction, not you. Why are we always talking like this? Something wrong with our horoscopes . . .'

'Your horoscope and the tiger's seem to be better matched,' she would say.

'Don't talk in that style. Someday you will be sorry that you have disturbed my mind. You don't realize that I need a calm mind and concentration in my work. My mood must not be spoilt . . .'

'As if I don't need a calm mind in my job! You think only of yourself and your tiger.'

I don't know why she was measuring herself against me all the time. Fancy anyone being jealous of a tiger! Yet it was not really so. Given her chance, I don't think she would have poisoned me. She enjoyed being argumentative, that's all. They were a peculiar couple, devoted to each other but not betraying their feelings in speech. When I mentioned this subject to my Master, later in life, and sought his verdict as to whether they were to be considered friendly or inimical to each other, he just smiled and said, 'Human ties cannot be defined in just black-and-white terms. There can be no such thing as unmitigated hatred or unmitigated love. Those who are deeply attached sometimes deliberately present a rough exterior to each other and that is also one way of enjoying the married state. Some wives in this world show their deepest love only by nagging, and the husbands also enjoy putting on an air of being victims. You must not forget that everyone is acting a part all the time, knowingly or unknowingly. But God who sees everything must be aware of their thoughts and the secret ecstasies of companionship of even that Captain and his wife . . . So don't make the mistake of thinking that they were not properly matched, judging merely from conversation overheard.' Do you know, at the end, though his death was sudden, with the last flicker of consciousness he worried about his wife and how she was going to manage without him. Do you know what she did when she came over and saw him? She stood looking at the body without a word or a tear; and when others tried to comfort her said, 'Leave me alone.' After that she went back to the circus tent, climbed to the top where the swings were clamped, took out one, took a full swing up and down, and when the swing touched the ceiling, let go her hold . . .

'Jubilee' seemed to have become a self-explanatory word. When Captain started the publicity for his special Jubilee Show, no one questioned it, although his wife continued to taunt him. Announcements were made through colourful lithographed posters pasted on every wall in Malgudi. You could find the posters stuck side by side, starting from Albert Mission College compound wall, the first available wall when you turned townward from the circus grounds, on which was originally to be seen the bold stencilled warning, BILL STICKERS WILL BE PROSECUTED. Captain's men had come back to consult him about it, and Captain advised, 'Stick the posters well over their warning and that will make it lawful . . . If we are questioned we shall send complimentary passes to the principal and professors.' He had planned to put up a few more special ringside seats to take care of all possible objectors and obstructors, from the sanitary department to the jail superintendent, who could have created trouble for Captain at any stage; though law-abiding in a general sense, he had contempt for what he felt were silly objections. This was not the time for one to be finicky. He had to make use of the sprawling Central Jail walls, paint over them his Jubilee messages in giant lettering so that travellers journeying on the highway could not miss them. He had always felt that such walls were going to waste and should be utilized properly. He differed from those whom he considered a bunch of eccentrics, calling themselves Town Arts Council, who were opposed to every kind of announcement and hoarding, never realizing that they were thus cramping our economic life and ultimate prosperity.

When his plans were opposed, he had his own technique of winning over opposition, a few complimentary tickets (not always for VIP seats; he had a few seats for semi-VIPs and non-VIPs, accommodation in rattan chairs, wooden chairs, and galleries, depending upon the status of those to be favoured). When mere tickets would not work, he donated cash from a fund he had earmarked as 'Birthday Gifts' in his account books, and Income Tax rarely questioned whose birthday. He invaded every blank space in town to advertise the Jubilee. Starting with Albert Mission College, as we have seen, to the end of Abu Lane which splintered off from Ellamman Street, the last outpost of Malgudi eastward, every kind of wall, of shops, schools, houses, and hotels, proclaimed the Jubilee of the Grand Malgudi Circus, displaying Rita in death-defying trapeze acts, the chimp riding a motor cycle, the tusker carrying on its back the chimp dressed as a Maharaja with crown and all, a giraffe doing something or the other, and clowns tumbling. At every corner people stood staring at the wall. Even those in a hurry to go to work paused to read the notice. Not a single soul was left in doubt about the coming Jubilee celebrations of the circus. In the same manner the countryside was also informed by the usual team of clowns with extra noise of drums.

As a result of this publicity, the box office presented an air of a besiegement on the opening day. Every inch of the auditorium was occupied for all the three shows each day – noon, evening and night.

Captain reserved the tiger's act for the night show. It came after Rita's trapeze act, somersaults, and dive through a fire ring. When the tiger was wheeled in and the enclosure was erected around the ring, Captain, dressed in satin breeches and a glittering vest, holding the whip in hand, appeared before the audience in a kind of light skipping movement, bowed to the public deeply in all directions, and introduced, 'Ladies and gentlemen, you are about to see our Raja perform an act which I have named "Four-in-One", which is actually a symphony in movement as you will notice when the band plays. I have composed it with a lot of forethought. It's a sequence of precise acts, timed properly, which sense of time is displayed uncannily by Raja. He will go through the act with precision, and finish the sequence as befits a country dedicated to non-violence, with a sip of milk in the company of a goat. I'd now appeal to you ladies and gentlemen to watch this act un-winkingly, keep your eyes open and your nerves cool – never fear for a moment that Raja will ever overstep the bounds in any manner.'

After this speech, which created suspense and anticipation in the audience, he let me out of the cage, opening the door with his own hand. He carried nothing more than his whip; he had put away even the chair. He wished to demonstrate that he was absolutely confident of his authority over me and had nothing to fear. He cracked his whip in the air twice to start me off. I galloped around the ring, while he watched with a side glance at his stop-watch, keeping himself deftly at a distance just a foot beyond my pouncing range, but always close to an emergency exit. The audience watched in absolute silence without stirring. I too caught the atmosphere and enjoyed showing off my talent. When the rounds were completed, the hurdles and mazes and labyrinths appeared at the appropriate places, and then rings of flames at some points, followed by the item of the goat and the milk. My mouth watered at the sight of the goat, but Captain was very careful to crack his whip and drive me back to the cage, unobtrusively, when he noticed it.

No one had witnessed such a composite and complex act before. When the applause subsided, Captain came forward and said, "Sorry, gentlemen, no encore is practical for this particular act, nor am I in a position to ask Raja to take the bow personally. I'll have to do it on his behalf. But I also hope someday I'll educate him in proper manners to respond to his adoring public.' And more applause . . .

The Four-in-One act and the fiery dive of the trapeze artistes were very popular and brought Captain great fame. His box-office collections soared, and apart from that his admirers showered on him cash and presents of all kinds. He had done something original and really creative in the annals of circus and no one could repeat or imitate his programme; the success was entirely due to Captain's genius. Jubilee, going on and on, each week bringing in more crowds than ever. Captain looked particularly happy and ordered an extra ration for all the animals every day. He was careful not to overfeed any animal that had, like myself, difficult acts to perform: 'Keep Raja light, and feed him well at the end of his act, late at night. If he becomes heavy, he won't be fit to run through his acts so smartly' – with the result that they hardly fed me until midnight, when all my duty was done. This compulsory fasting the whole day kept me always hungry, and made it more and more difficult to accept the milk in the goat's company.

Thus it went on day after day, week after week, for a very long time. One evening I had just gone through all the turns preceding the milk – run with and without hurdles and through fire – and was sitting before the pan of milk. As a piece of courtesy to a weaker companion, the goat must be allowed to sip the milk first. He now had great confidence in me and took me for granted – rather a risky thing to do. I sat up watching him, assuming as benign a look as possible since the slightest frown on my face might bring the whip down, Captain being watchful as ever. As the goat bent down and stretched its neck to reach the milk in the pan, I felt a powerful impulse to seize that smooth white neck held out so temptingly – the agony of self-control was worse than the raging hunger. The gluttonous goat was lapping up the milk. How lovely it'd be to put one's teeth to it and go off to the bamboo bush to a leisurely meal.

Forest memories overwhelmed me while that silly goat was relishing its milk, as if he had never tasted it before.

If only he had lifted his head, withdrawn even slightly, out of my reach, the world would have heard a different story. As it happened, the temptation stayed too long – holding myself back seemed impossible. Captain, reading my mind, was more alert that ever; he cracked his whip as a warning and commanded me to share the milk while the goat was still at it. But I hated that milk more than ever, and was delaying the unpleasant task. Normally when Captain fixed his look on me, I'd be nearly paralysed, and obey. But now, suddenly he had to look away, when he heard a commotion in the auditorium as someone fell off the top rung of a gallery. I chose this moment to shoot forward and nip off the goat's head. There were shouts and cries and confusion from a section nearby for a minute, and Captain whipped me hard, picked up his chair, hit me with it, and drove me back to my cage. The goat was finished, but of no use to me whatever, as it was snatched away out of sight at once and the place was cleaned and cleared as if nothing unusual had happened. Among the several thousands in the hall, a handful in the front row had noticed the end of the goat, but they were dignified VIPs who would not normally scream even if they noticed a fire or murder. Before the general spectators in the hall could know what was happening, I was back in my cage. The men had cleared the place very quickly, efficient men behind a curtain drawn all around, and the next item came on without delay as if nothing had happened. Four of our best clowns, along with the chimp in tuxedo and wearing spectacles, came on the stage with their special charms and jugglery, and completely diverted the minds of the audience so that no question was asked as to how the preceding item had ended.

Meanwhile I must say I had become unpopular with Captain. He shunned me for a few days and dropped my acts completely from his announcements, explaining to the audience in one of his speeches, 'Ladies and gentlemen, I'm sorry to say that Raja's acts have to be suspended for a few days as he has distemper and needs rest and isolation.'

'Rest and isolation' meant starving to me. They gave me neither food nor water for three days on end, Captain's usual method of chastening one's temper. I wished I could have explained that what I had done was due to robust health and hunger and in no way to be described as distemper. Distemper indeed! If they had left me alone, I could have helped them forget the existence of the goat completely. At least they should have let me finish off my prize; I had thought I would take it to my cage . . . What right did he have to starve me? I felt enraged at the thought of Captain and his allies and wished the iron bars could yield, and then I could show them another way to celebrate the Jubilee. The isolation hurt me most. I had got used to the company of that wonderful chimp and all the good fellows, gossiping among ourselves from our confinements or tether posts. However, the chimp sneaked in beside my cage unobserved when Captain was away on some business in the town and the keepers were relaxing. He said, 'What had come over you?'

'I was hungry, that's all,' I said.

'How can you eat a friend with whom you had been on milk-drinking terms, however hungry you might be! Though I am sorry for the poor goat, for he was mild and inoffensive, I'm glad to say that it's done us some good. Captain is talking of closing the Jubilee shows and resting for a few days. I was there when he was talking to his wife at breakfast and she said, "The first wise act in your life . . . We are all at breaking point, I'm sure." He didn't dispute her remark as he normally would, but remained moody and gave me a cup of tea to wash down a buttered toast. It was so good. Why can't you also eat these things, so much better than your normal preferences . . . You'll be a good fellow if you learn to eat things that don't move or breathe, and then people will not blame you, but accept you in society and have you around without

[66]

these iron bars. Then you will be popular, not feared. If you are hungry, I can bring you a banana and some nuts sometimes. Many visitors bring me a lot – I can't eat all of it . . .'

Listening to him made me feel worse. I said, 'Don't talk about food, unless you can get me what I can eat. It's no use talking about it. Your talk makes my hunger worse . . .' And the chimp went away with a leer. I was in no mood for jokes.

I suffered hunger another day. When I was lying half-dead Captain came up, peered in through the bars, and said to his companion, 'Take a look at him now. Not at his best. He is under treatment for his misconduct. I hope he has learnt a lesson . . .'

'Put up another goat before him and see what he can do. That was a magnificent shot I took in sixteen-millimetre. I was lucky to be there in time to take it. I don't think you could ever repeat it. One-in-a-million situation . . . As I watched, he was so quick no one could have noticed his action. His head shot up like a cobra's and he just pecked at that goat . . . but it was like a – it was snap-action, neat, precise like a surgeon's . . .' That man was so full of enthusiasm and praise for me that he became incoherent and could hardly complete a sentence.

Captain said, 'So what?'

'You don't seem to appreciate it . . . It'd be an impossible, un-believably perfect shot – the kind of thing that a film director would be dreaming about. I shall treasure the shot I've taken and use it somewhere, and if it gets an award in any international film show, don't be surprised . . .'

'Raja is my tiger, and I want a royalty for a show by him . . .'

The other laughed as if he had heard a humorous statement, and then said, 'Captain, ever since I saw Raja's surgical performance on the goat, I have been thinking of a story in which I could put him to proper use . . .'

'I have to think it over,' said the Captain. 'I can't give an instant yes or no. I want two days.'

[67]

'But I can't force you to give a reply. Think it over, and understand that I can give you a handsome offer . . . but don't starve him further. Feed him. He is magnificent; don't spoil him. You have no idea how he will look in colour.' He took another long look at me and said, 'Raja the Great. I am sure you will cooperate with us . . .'

Both of them went away. I heard the tinkling of the bucket handle and stood expectantly. My food was come. An attendant placed meat and water in the other half of the cage, locked it, and pulled open the partition. I gave a roar of pleasure, and attained a feeling of well-being very soon. I was able to pace up and down the entire length of the cage in a happy state of mind.

Captain spoke to his wife about the film-maker that night. After the Jubilee he was going through a period of rest for two weeks before starting preparations to move on to Trichy, the next camp. This was just the time when Captain could enjoy a little domestic felicity. Go to bed early and find time to talk to his wife. When he mentioned the film proposal she asked, 'What exactly is Raja expected to do?'

'I'll know it soon, but I must know first of all whether we should consider the proposal at all . . .'

'I'll say nothing until I know what you are going to say.'

'Why?'

'So that I may save you the trouble of contradicting me.'

They were in a pleasant mood of banter without acrimony or any relevance. She asked, 'Can they handle Raja?'

'They can't. The idea seems to be that they will tell me what they want, and I get Raja to do it.'

She remained in deep thought for a while and said, 'I don't know, I've always hated that brute . . . seems undependable . . . I feel uneasy whenever you are out with him.'

Captain laughed at her fears. 'Let me say he is more docile than a

Siamese cat . . . However, I'm not asking for a testimonial, but whether we should consider the film proposal at all.'

'Yes, if he will buy this little cat off your hands . . .'

'Nothing of the kind, my dear, I won't part with him as long as I run a circus. I'm looking for another goat to train; until then Raja can be used elsewhere.'

'Another poor goat to be made into a ghost?' was all that she could say. 'Shocking it was. I realized that if you relax even for a split second he'll, God knows what he will do . . . the way he glares! I feel more easy with your lions . . . they are noble and gentle – I don't know why you should not be satisfied with their work, and want to bother about this tiger or any tiger . . .'

'Given a chance the lion can also bifurcate a goat. Don't take too harsh a view of Raja for it . . . He didn't do it out of malevolence, but a sudden impulse of mischief. That's a way of life in their jungle society.'

'What an explanation!' she cried. 'I don't know if you will ever listen to me.'

'All the time I do nothing but listen. Anyway, the main question is whether Raja should be lent for film work at all. However, there is time to think it over. Instead of idling his time . . .'

The film-maker, whose visiting card, embossed on a thin sandalwood strip that filled Captain's office with fragrance, said, 'Madhusudan, Cine-Director and Producer', came in as promised on the third day.

Captain said, 'The scent of your visiting card heralds your arrival even before you appear.'

'That's my intention, Captainji. If you keep it in your table drawer, you will not forget me. Call me Madan.'

Captain showed him a chair. 'I'm a TT, but I can get you a drink, if you would like that sort of thing . . .'

'Never touch a drop when I have to talk business.'

'Why?' asked Captain. 'I thought for people like you it'd sharpen your negotiations.'

'No, sir, I should like to be aware of what I'm saying,' said the director.

Captain engaged him in small talk for a while, called for soft drinks, and said, 'Now let me hear your proposal.'

The director cleared his throat and lit a cigarette. 'It's a simple one. Ever since I saw your tiger, I wanted to make a picture with him in the chief role. I have watched his performance for weeks now, while the idea was developing in my mind. But when I saw him the other evening so neatly slicing the goat, I said to myself, "Ah, here is my material, here is what I have been seeking eternally. I'm at the end of the quest."'

'The tip of the rainbow where the golden bowl is!' added Captain.

'You are absolutely right, sir,' cried the director. 'So you understand me! You are a genius, sir.'

Captain cried, 'You are no less so, now go on. We understand each other.'

The director said, 'Ever since I saw that act of your tiger in relation to the goat, I felt inspired, particularly after I saw the shot in sixteen-millimetre, which of course is going to be blown up to thirty-five and integrated in the feature, and, oh, boy! it's going to be a sensation.'

Captain, being used to the company of monologists, sat patiently without fidgeting or interrupting the other's flow of talk as he went on dilating on his aesthetic and commercial outlook without coming near any actual offer. When he had gone on for fifteen minutes, Captain felt he should put in a sentence of his own lest the other take him to be asleep, and said: 'You found the goat scene inspiring, but my wife Rita, although accustomed to circus life, felt sickened by the spectacle and retired; even now when she recollects the scene, she is in tears . . .'

The other said, 'Of course, women are likely to be squeamish, and we have to make allowances for that, but we can't allow our plans to be guided by them. I always take care to see that when my picture goes up for the censor's certificate it is seen only by the male members on the panel . . . After all the film medium is where Art and Commerce meet – we have to keep that fact always in mind. All the sentimentalists' outcry against the so-called sex and violence must be ignored. They make too much out of it. Life is created and made possible only through sex and violence, no use fighting against it, shutting one's eyes to the facts of life . . . Inspired by your circus act I sat up that night and wrote the outline of the story in which Raja would be the main feature. The human side in the story will be a hero called Jaggu. I have already booked him; he was an all-in wrestler and physical-feats performer and weighs one hundred kilogrammes, two metres in height. When he is photographed, his figure will fill a wide screen. I had booked him and was looking for a story. I was lucky to have got one of your VIP seats at the show, through a friend in the Collector's office – that's how I was able to film the goat sequence.'

'I didn't notice your camera . . . I'd not have permitted it.'

'I know, I know, I wouldn't blame you. But I've a special kind of camera, which can't be noticed . . . What was I saying?'

'Your last sentence ringing in my ear is "Goat sequence . . ."'

'Thank you. The goat, brought up as a pet, is constantly being pursued by the tiger, who is accustomed to ripping off goat heads, but the giant who owns the goat fights it off with his bare hands. He finally captures the tiger and trains it to live at peace with the goat . . . Non-violence is India's contribution to civilization. I got the idea from your own speech before the tiger act; violence can be conquered only by non-violence . . .'

'Then how are you going to fit in the shot you have already taken?'

The director became thoughtful. 'I'll get a story writer to fix all that. After all it should be his business. How can you show non-violence without showing a lot of violence and how bad it is?'

'Sex, how about it?' Captain was enjoying this talk. He found it relaxing after all the strenuous labour of recent days.

'Oh, yes, that part of the story will come through in our story conference and the story writer should be able to work it in properly. Everyone knows how important normal sex is and what an evil sex can turn out to be without a proper philosophy of life.'

'With a virile giant running about, it should not be difficult for him to hunt women also . . . Well, that part of it cannot concern me – only the tiger. If we agree on terms and if you would complete Raja's part of the work within the time I specify, it'll suit me.'

'I don't know . . . If there should be any retakes?'

'We'll think of it. But let us discuss terms, if we may . . .'

'I hope you will not demand too much. I want your cooperation and encouragement. We are planning on a moderate budget, getting the technicians and crew from Madras, shooting mostly outdoors . . .'

'I can spare Raja for two weeks at the start and for retake extensions, we'll see, we may have to think of special terms . . .'

'What are your terms? You are mentioning only special terms.'

'Meet me again three days from now. I'll have to talk to my lawyer.'

'There should be no delay . . . We must shoot in the bright season. I am anxious to start the production without delay. I have come to you because you are an animal lover like me; with your cooperation I want to make an international picture. I'm not having a dialogue writer yet, I want to try how far we can go with a minimum of speech, which should make the picture appreciable anywhere in the world . . . I am young – I want your blessing,' he appealed.

[72]

'I'm not a hermit to give blessings. I'm only a businessman, and expect my terms to be fulfilled if my services are wanted.'

At which Madan threw open his briefcase, took out a cheque-book and a pen, poised the point over the cheque, and said, 'Mention your figure and I'll put it down and sign. I'm also a businessman.'

Captain watched him calmly with a smile. 'Put it back. I don't accept a cheque. Anyway, I have said see me again and we can discuss terms. On Friday you will have my terms neatly written down. You will have only to put your signature to it, and then you may schedule your work.'

It sounded simple enough, but Madan found it difficult to conclude the transaction. He could not understand what Captain expected him to do to finalize the business. He came almost every morning. He was staying at The Travellers' Bungalow, four miles out, and had to visit the circus camp every day. He had to be satisfied with meeting Anand, who would keep him seated in his office, offer him coffee and soft drinks but no interview with the boss: 'He is in the training enclosure,' which implied that no one could reach him or watch him at work. Captain knew it was hard on the creature under training, and did not want any sentimental busybody to watch and carry tales to the SPCA. Any visitor who strayed beyond the STRICTLY KEEP OUT board faced the danger of being thrown out.

It made Madan fret while waiting in the front office. 'Do you realize that I have to come five miles each day and go back, while all my technical arrangements are ready, but unutilized?' Anand never paid attention to his complaints, but went on with his work at the desk, answering him in monosyllables, and if the visitor seemed too impatient, silencing him with refreshments. Anand just said, 'When he is rehearsing, even I cannot approach him, even if the tent should be on fire.'

'How long should one wait?'

'That I can't say . . . Sometimes he goes on for eight hours at a stretch. Unless the performer executes what he has in mind, he never lets go. It may take a whole day.'

'So how long should I wait?'

'That I can't say . . . In this season of training for the next camp, he is generally not available; even his wife can't disturb him.'

'Can I go and watch the tiger in the cage, please?'

'Yes, of course, but we have to have the boss's permission.'

'But you can't reach him.'

'Yes, that's true,' Anand said sadly, which was not helpful in any way.

Madan sat every day at Anand's office for four hours at a stretch, while Anand went about his business at his desk and also outside, leaving Madan alone. Madan soon tired of waiting, bored with the outdated newspapers and illustrated magazines on the table. He felt outraged. He told Anand one day, 'I'm a businessman too, sir. I have other things to do than just sit waiting for a *darshan* of the great man.'

Anand said with a smile, 'You must not get discouraged. Many others have had to wait for weeks to see him. After all, in business matters, one should be calm . . .'

At which Madan lost his temper, stamped his foot, and started shouting. The uproar brought Captain on the scene. He asked, 'What is going on?' Madan started a harangue, a long narrative full of indignation. Captain cut it short by saying, as if nothing had happened, neither apologetic nor explaining anything, 'Come, come, let us adjourn to my room.'

Madan followed him sheepishly, grateful that he could at last have an audience. He opened his briefcase, sending out a whiff of sandalwood perfume from his special visiting cards. He took out a sheet of paper. 'Here is my proposal in writing. Please say what you want.'

Captain glanced through the proposal and said, 'Not suitable. I'm only giving you my tiger for a set purpose, for a limited period, and not surrendering him to you. You will have to re-draft the whole thing.'

Madan was aghast. 'Nowhere have I said –'

Captain did not allow him to continue. 'That's all right. Please listen to my advice, and all will be well . . . It's better we have it out at this stage, rather than later – possibly in a courtroom.'

'Oh, I hate to have anything to do with lawyers or courts,' Madan said nervously.

But Captain said, 'I don't mind such things. In my profession, all the time I have to think of lawyers and courts. Can't help it, if I must survive.'

Madan was slightly frightened and completely softened by this time. He took back his document and said, 'Captain-*sab*, give me a draft and I'll sign it blindfold . . . Only tell me when to come, so that –'

'So that you don't waste your time? Mr Madan, my time is not my own. My work lies in getting things done with the cooperation of all sorts of animals . . . and I've to depend upon their time. Anyway, let us say next Friday, at ten o'clock. I'll try to keep myself free, and keep away from the animals.' And he laughed as if it were a joke.

Before leaving Madan pleaded, 'The technical unit are waiting for a word from us. I can't hold them off indefinitely . . .'

'Next Friday at ten o'clock,' said Captain repeatedly, and showed him the door.

Several days had to pass before Madan could finalize the agreement. Captain would not be available, or if available would disagree with some clause and send the document back for re-drafting.

'You see, the artiste [they were referring to Raja] should be present at the location when called.'

'No, sir, you have to be specific about time and place. Suppose you have a location in Timbuctoo . . .'

Madan looked desperate. 'If it was to be at Timbuctoo, why would I be here, sir?'

'I don't know, I want you to be specific. I don't mean Timbuctoo literally, of course . . .'

'I have not yet fixed the location.'

'Why don't you do that first? From what I see you are ready only with the tiger . . . Not adequate for the starting.'

'I've Jaggu, the hero of the story; I've booked him and he is staying with me – won't let him out of sight till the picture is completed. I'll keep him for possible retakes too.'

'Excellent, your actors are ready, but not your stage.'

'Each day's delay is costing –'

'Don't bother to tell me the figures or your calculations. I've enough calculations of my own, God knows . . .' He glanced at his watch. 'Now I have to be off, my friend. Come again with practical ideas . . .'

'When? When?' Madan asked anxiously. There could be no specific answer to it; he was not even sure these days about the tiger – a fundamental doubt. Every time he suggested that he should be allowed to watch the tiger, he was put off with some objection or other, until Madan began to wonder if he was to get the real tiger or a stuffed one. In his feverish thinking, anything seemed possible. But it was too late to back out of the project. He had taken custody of the strong man Jaggu, who sat placidly in the front veranda of The Travellers' Bungalow, swatting flies, which somehow were attracted to him in swarms. The technical crew awaiting his orders at Madras kept demanding action. He flourished letters and telegrams from them in the hope of impressing Captain. But Captain viewed them indifferently, only remarking, 'After all, technicians are there for our use, not the other way round. Don't let the tail wag the dog. Be firm. They must realize who is the boss; they must not try to rule us. You are a good fellow, full of enterprise – don't be weak in management. You must work on bases which are firm. You know, Dadhaji used to say . . .' He would quote some significant aphorism concerning business management.

Madan felt desperate; when he succeeded in securing an audience with the great man, it was difficult to keep him to the point. He could not make out what Captain was to gain by delaying like this. When he tried to be strict, Captain would just say, 'Madan, my friend, know this, I won't be coerced whatever may happen. You bring the answers to my queries, and then you'll have my green signal. It must go on at its own pace. Why should we hurry? I won't be coerced or hustled; and I am quite prepared to drop the whole proposal, if you cannot satisfy my conditions. First fix your location, and then come to me.'

'Can't you help me?'

'No,' said Captain with an air of finality. 'It should be your business and your technicians', not mine.'

This placed a big strain on the film producer. The greater the urgency he showed, the more Captain delayed, until he felt challenged and got into a fever of activity which did not cease night or day. When he reappeared before Captain a few days later, he was able to be specific about three locations. The first one was rejected because it was close to the jungle, and Captain explained, 'Psychologically unsound, as the tiger may become homesick and behave queerly, if not desert us.' He rejected the second location, an open ground across river Sarayu, beyond Nallappa Grove, for the reason that it was too close to the town and might attract crowds. The third location, in the southern direction, a wooded area, where the highway passed within a couple of furlongs, was finally approved, and the contract was signed. Madan felt as triumphant as if he had produced a picture and received the Oscar.

Madan worked night and day to transform the land he had taken on lease – a place which had somehow come to be known as the Ginger Field, possibly because at some remote period someone had cultivated ginger and sent up the crop in wagon-loads for extraction to a factory in Madras, and later sold the land to a pawnbroker at the Market Gate. Madan lost no time in preparing the location for shooting. He engaged men and women from a near-by village to remove stones and bumps, and sweep and smooth out the ground. He pressed Jaggu into service, a welcome diversion for him from swatting flies at The Travellers' Bungalow. He uprooted boulders and tossed them off with ease. He lifted heavy articles in the construction of sets (a village street with a row of two-dimensional homes), stockades, and platforms for mounting lights, reflectors, cameras.

When all was ready, Madan could persuade Captain to come up and see it, and felt happy when Captain remarked after his inspection, 'You are truly great to be able to transform Ginger Field into a film studio.'

'All your blessing and cooperation,' Madan replied.

'More than mine, seems to be that giant's cooperation,' said Captain. 'He is, I suppose, a substitute for power-lifts, steam hammers, cranes, and other stuff of that kind.'

'He could carry down that generator as if it were a box of matches. Hauls up stacks of bamboos for the fencing, probably a ton at a time, he just picked them up and set them in place . . . For all his appearance, he is mild and gentle.'

Captain cast a special eye on the spot chosen for the tiger, and suggested a few changes: 'Get the enclosure close upon this spot, so that the cage is not hit by the evening sun, which is not good for the tiger. Give me twenty-four hours' notice, and I'll have him ready for your call. Your Jaggu is really a find,' he said, looking at him while he was unloading a truck-load of property and enjoying the task. 'What a mountain of a man! You are lucky. I could have used him in my circus too – for lifting and moving which goes on all the time with twenty hands at the job. After you have done with him, will you please let me try him?'

'Of course, if you like. After all the possible retakes, when the negatives are cut, I'll set him free and you may have him. Perhaps if you include an all-in wrestling show, he'll excel in that . . .'

'Oh, that may not fit into my general programming, but I'll take him on and see what I can do.'

Madan explained, 'I first saw him at a village market fair. I was travelling from Trichy to Madras, and owing to a tyre-burst and a radiator leak the car stalled at an awkward place, and had to be taken to a wayside mechanic. The nearest village smithy was over a mile away, but everyone was at the weekly market fair when I went along to seek help. At the fair I noticed this fellow standing on a little platform and challenging the people around to come up and wrestle, even four at a time, if they chose. When his challenge was accepted, and a batch of four fell on him, he just brushed them off with the back of his hand. His admirers applauded and cheered, while his challengers picked themselves up from the dust and paid down the wager. That seemed to be his main source of income. The money was collected by a woman; I learned from the crowd that she was his wife. Bouts of wrestling were followed by feats of strength: he snapped chains, bent and twisted iron rods, split a slab of granite with the edge of his palm, and even offered to run a road engine over his chest if someone could arrange it. The puny wife went round collecting money. Now, after his performance, I took him along to the spot where my car had stopped, and he just pushed it down the road like a perambulator. I paid ten rupees to his wife and they were overwhelmed. Before he returned to his place at the fair, I noted down his address. He lived in a hut and made money at the market fairs in the countryside. While I was brooding on a subject for a film, the sight of this man gave me an idea for a "strong-man" story of a giant who could not be contained. When I went back that way again, I visited his hut and offered him five hundred rupees a month for one year with food (that was most important) to join me and do whatever role I gave him. His puny wife was delighted to let him go, having never seen so much money in her life. Her condition was that he'd send her money every month and get back to her at the end of it all. After I saw the tiger act in your circus, I wanted to combine them in my story – and there we are.'

They were seated on folding chairs in the shade of a large banyan tree. Captain looked happy and relaxed, much to Madan's relief – very different from what he seemed at the circus ground. Madan asked, 'Would you like a cup of coffee, tea, or fruit juice?'

'You have all that here too?' Captain exclaimed patronizingly.

'First thing I arranged to have was the canteen over there, where you see the smoke – otherwise no work would go on here; they'll be going out all the time for a refreshing drink ... For stronger refreshments too they have a tavern – fortunately for us a mile out of here – where I believe they gather at the end of the day. I don't let them leave this spot during their working hours ... though sometimes I notice some transaction going on across the barrier at the back of the lot ...'

'Don't notice too much. You must know when not to be too observant. I have a team of about three hundred at work, I find all sorts of problems. I can't be too strict or rigid as long as they do their work, I try not to look too closely ...'

Captain was relaxed; Madan felt expansive and said, 'You will be welcome to come and spend as much time as you like here ... You look more happy here.'

The make-up and costume section was in one of the huts, and it could hardly hold the make-up man and his assistants as Jaggu stood in the centre. He was fitted with a leopard-skin covering, which was strapped across his shoulder; his hair was tousled so that it stood like an aura, and they had given him a moustachio, which curved up to his ears. There had been a controversy among the make-up men whether the ends should curve down in pirate fashion or up like a colonel's. They went on arguing about it so hotly that Madan heard their wrangling from under the shade of his banyan tree and came over to ask what the matter was; he stood at the entrance, impressed with the mighty figure, while the make-up men were going round him like pygmies. They went on touching him up here and there as if he were inanimate. Except for a little shifting of his legs, and letting out a deep sigh, he gave no sign of being alive. Madan studied him and cried, 'Here, pull off those moustaches. He is all right plain-faced. He is like Tarzan and not like a pirate or Bhima.'

'But, sir, there must be some break-up or offset for his face. It's too plain for the large area . . .'

'It's sticky, sir, and scratching, sir,' mumbled Jaggu through the gum on his lips.

'Where did you get the idea to give him whiskers? Take them off immediately,' Madan ordered while Jaggu looked on gratefully. 'Also loosen his robe a bit – it should come down to his knees, even covering his knees. Otherwise, it will look as if he wore a loincloth, and will cut a sorry figure on the screen – enough material in that cloak, loosen all the pleats . . .' It took them over two hours before achieving the results visualized by Madan. Pulling out the moustache was ticklish, literally, and Jaggu moaned and wriggled and was reprimanded by Madan's assistant supervising the operations.

Finally at about nine o'clock the hero was ready: properly painted and costumed, his hair done up in proper style. Madan and his assistant stood around gazing and commenting.

Madan looked satisfied. 'An hour or more wasted because of the moustache. I don't know where they got the idea from – our mythology, I suppose! Jaggu is not a demon . . . We must establish him as a normal human being. Any character with whiskers repels – particularly women and children. Polanski has explained somewhere ['Who is Polanski?' the assistant wanted to ask, but checked himself] the audience's sympathy must be established first – and he has statistics to show that between a character with hair on his lip and one clean-shaven, the latter gains more sympathy . . .' His assistants stood around nodding appreciatively at his knowledge of the *shastras* of cinematography. Madan looked with admiration while Jaggu was brought out. He said, 'Go up to that hut. Let us see how you do it. Walk naturally . . . don't swing your arms . . . be natural. Camera rehearsal,' he shouted suddenly and a cameraman suddenly sprang into action. 'O.K., boss, a little more to the left, please . . . more left . . .'

They made Jaggu return to the starting point, marked it with white paint, and told him to walk up again to the steps of the first cottage. They measured the distance with a tape and marked a circle on the cottage step, and directed him to stand in that circle with his back to the camera. The director ordered, 'Don't turn until you hear a cry, "Tiger, Tiger!" Till that cry is heard don't move even an inch . . .' He was made to walk back and forth repeatedly. He began to perspire and pant, and tried to wipe his forehead, at which a great cry went up, 'Oh, no, don't wipe!' and a make-up man dashed up to him and dabbed his face with a towel, and touched it up. Then he was made to stand within the circle with his back to them. 'Don't turn. Stare ahead until you hear the shout, "Tiger! Tiger!" Do you follow me?'

'Yes, sir.'

The director allowed a pause and suddenly screamed, 'Tiger! Tiger!'

'Where?' Jaggu asked involuntarily in a stentorian voice, looking around in panic: he made a move to spring forward.

The director cried, 'Idiot! I told you not to move out of this mark. Get back and stay there . . .' This slight exercise disrupted all the original arrangement. Once again they brought all the measuring tape and stretched it between the starting point and the circle. The cameraman kept saying, 'More left, more left, your feet in the circle . . . Now come forward just one foot . . .' Someone came up and held a meter close to his cheek again and went back, and the make-up man was again patting his cheeks with a cotton swab. Jaggu felt tired and confused. Madan said to his assistant, 'He must be told the sequence of this scene.'

He approached Jaggu as he stood with his back to them, and went round to face him. 'Now don't move, only listen. They will now take a shot standing as you are now. Following it, you will hear the cry "Tiger! Tiger!" When that's heard, you will only say, "Ah!" as loudly as you can, spin round like this, raise your arm and spring forward with a war-cry and run up to that starting point over there marked white, demolish the tiger and walk back casually . . .' Madan demonstrated every detail of his advice, spinning round with upraised arm and falling forward. He showed the action repeatedly till Jaggu could understand, and then withdrew to his chair marked 'Director', called for a glass of water, and sipping it said, 'Handling this idiot is proving more difficult than I had expected. However, I'm determined . . . Tell them to be ready to shoot in five minutes. Is the clap ready, "Shot One Take One"? Check it. Sound and camera . . . ready . . . sequence number . . .'

While this was going on a cry was heard from the other end of the field: 'Tiger has come!' On hearing it Jaggu without any warning spun round with a great cry and sprang forward with his arms upraised. A couple of members of the crew who were on duty jumped out of his way to avoid his stormy approach. Madan tore his hair in despair and demanded, 'Who cried that?'

'The tiger carriage has come, sir, and they are now bringing the carriage down the field, sir,' explained one.

Madan looked at the cameraman and said, 'Bloody mess . . .

Begin all over again.' He said to his assistant, 'Take that fool back to his position. Keep him within the circle. Let him not budge even a hair's breadth ... Otherwise tell him he will be sacked. Touch him up all over again ...' At this moment, Captain arrived in his small car. Madan rose to receive him.

From my cage I could watch the scene and also hear a great deal of their conversation after their mutual greetings. I felt happy to be able to stay in this wood. It reminded me of my jungle days and revived a craving for freedom. I couldn't complain of anything now; I was protected and fed and looked after by Captain. But that seemed hardly to suffice. I'd enjoy being able to move about and exercise my limbs as I pleased. Though well kept, I was still a prisoner. If only they could trust me and open the door, I'd go out, run, and return to my cage. But my species has an unfortunate reputation, and one's natural actions are misconstrued. People talk ill of us all the time. It's our misfortune that neither the denizens of the jungle nor those of the towns would trust us or behave boldly – the exception being Captain, but he had his own limitations of understanding: he had a wrong philosophy of depending upon the whip and his terrible voice, not realizing that I could be made to go through all those meaningless motions even without all that violence, by just being told what to do. But how to make him or anyone understand that his style drives one into a panic, and that left alone a tiger could be as innocent and harmless as a cow or a chimp?

I heard Madan say to Captain, 'This is what I want. It is up to you to arrange it. Raja must make one spring at Jaggu, who will ward it off with the back of his hand, and pound his face with such a cry that Raja will turn back with his tail between his legs.'

'Tucking the tail between legs should be more a dog's habit ... I've never seen any Felis species doing that.'

'But I want it so, it's in the script.'

'Change the script,' said Captain crisply. 'However, what's so important about the tail business?'

'It enhances the prestige of the hero, if he can make a tiger lower his tail in deference and crawl . . .'

'Who wrote the script?'

'Well, I did, who else could conceive it? I never allow anyone else to handle the basic script.'

'Why don't you talk to the tiger about it? He is over there. Take your script and read it to him and if he agrees I'll have absolutely no objection.'

Madan looked desperate and upset. 'Captain, you are kidding. This is not how I expect you to cooperate, I didn't grudge the full cash payment in advance you wanted for four weeks of shooting . . .'

'Tut, tut, don't talk like a moneylender. I've brought the tiger as agreed in our contract. I'll open the cage and bring him out to wrestle with your hero . . . I'll release him any moment you say you are ready.'

Their talk was interrupted by a plaintive appeal from the giant. 'I can't keep standing any longer. I want to rest. At least let me sit down on the floor.'

'Hey, stop that. I won't have you moan like this every minute, you are not a baby, not by any means, sir; I'll sack and sue you for damages if you do not cooperate. It's against the contract . . .'

'I'm tired,' wailed the giant.

The cameraman came to his rescue. 'No harm, sir, if he sits down, we have marked the place; it'll only take a few minutes to adjust again. Anyway we have been behind the camera since the morning, not a single shot. Light is changing – new measurements will be needed.'

One from a high platform said, 'What are we all supposed to be doing here?'

'Is this a protest meeting? Revolt, Rebellion, Rioting or what?'

asked Madan haughtily. 'If it is, tell me, and I know how to deal with mutineers. Don't you see we are in a discussion, and I can't proceed without a proper discussion. I won't be coerced under any circumstance; remember that discussion is the most important part of film-making. I don't have to explain to you all that . . .'

'It is not in the contract, and so naturally you don't have to explain to us why our time is being wasted!' remarked the cameraman cynically.

Madan ignored him for a moment, but said as if on an inspiration, 'I'm buying your time. If there is talk of waste, it's only my money.'

Captain felt that it was time to end this squabble. He appealed to the cameraman. 'You are an experienced man and you know how difficult is the film medium; it's where Art and Commerce are combined, as our friend here always says, and it suffers from the disadvantages of both. Once you are caught in it, you are finished. You can go neither back nor forward. That is the situation in which our friend finds himself now. So be patient. We will decide very soon how best to proceed, having come thus far . . .'

'But sir, we like to get on with the work . . .'

'That's of course a good idea. But you know, as an ace cameraman, how difficult it is to get artistes to do right! Here we have no normal actors, but a tiger and one who understands less than a tiger . . . Difficult work, but Madan has invested money and time. You must do your best for him and leave it to him to work it out.'

'But, sir, we have positioning and rehearsing again and again. Is there no limit? No wonder the artiste is half-dead. Actually we started at . . .'

A man from the top platform added, 'Before seven – and nothing done for four hours, while I'm perched here . . .'

'What can I do? Some fool gave the "Tiger" cue at a wrong moment.'

[86]

'You had asked me to keep a look-out for the arrival of the animal, sir, and I did it, that's all. I don't like to be called a fool.'

'Silence, no back-talk,' ordered Madan. 'I don't appreciate it.'

Captain continued his good offices, and announced, 'Coffee break.'

Immediately the atmosphere cleared and relaxed. The crew left their posts happily and swarmed around the canteen, Jaggu foremost among them. Madan watched them all helplessly, and protested, 'Too early for a break. They have not done an iota of work . . .'

'Not their fault really, but let us not go into all that now. One has to be flexible when dealing with workers. I know, because I have to contend with three hundred workers and animals of various sorts . . .'

While the crew were away refreshing themselves, Madan and Captain engaged in a discussion. 'Madan, I wish to help you, understand that. Stop all that nonsense about Raja's tail. Raja's face should be more important.'

'But at some point we must follow the script . . .'

'You mention it as if it were your scripture rather than your script. We will come to that later. Be clear as to what you want Raja to do before he tucks his tail.'

'He must stand up on his hind legs and place his forelegs on the giant's shoulder first. Then the giant will knock him off . . .'

'Marvellous conception!' commented Captain. 'In all my years of association with wild creatures –' He began his sentence and stopped short. 'Does it occur to you at all – that even granting that it's possible, the flesh on that poor fellow's shoulders is likely to be torn out, if nothing worse happens?'

'I depend on you . . . Can't you pull out his nails?'

'Horrible idea! Never.'

'But they will grow again . . . that's what they do in Hollywood.'

'Why don't you go to Hollywood then?'

[87]

'I want to make a hundred-per-cent Indian film. I have taken it as a challenge.'

'Who is challenging you?' asked Captain. 'Leaving the nail-pulling alone, that's not the worst to happen. Raja may decapitate your giant as he did that goat, an act which you so much admired.' Madan was lost in thought. Captain continued, 'I'll tell you right now, I won't have his teeth pulled out either. I can't think of it. Let me tell you even if everything is pulled out, Raja could still deliver a concussion with a pat. I want Raja to be restored to me in his original condition after the film shooting. If you look closely, you will find it in our contract. If there is a scar or mutilation on Raja, I'll sue for damages up to ten million dollars in your Hollywood terms.'

'Then, in some jungle pictures, what they do is to sew up the lips temporarily — the sutures are easily removed later. That's what they do in Hollywood.'

'To hell with Hollywood and stitches and sutures. The tiger must be returned intact.'

By this time the sun was going down. And the crew, who had returned to their posts and were watching, asked through their spokesman, 'Shall we pack up?'

'Yes, pack up,' cried Madan commandingly. He turned to Captain and said, 'You must cooperate with me, sir.'

'Yes, of course, you have lost a full day, and you will have one day less and I want you to do something worthwhile within the stipulated time.'

'Won't you give a little extension?'

'No, our circus is on the move, you know that. I have to send Raja off in advance . . . I'll tell you what we might do. You must utilize the flexibility of the film medium. On my side I'll make Raja stand on his hind legs and place his forepaws on a wrestler who is not there, and you will ask your giant to imagine himself to wrestle with a tiger which is not there. After all he was a wrestler and it

[88]

must not be difficult for him to imagine an adversary and pound him . . . Shoot them separately and join them through an optical printer. That way it should be easy to show them hugging . . .'

'Marvellous idea,' cried Madan. 'Next four days, we'll shoot the maximum footage. I'll get a second unit from Madras immediately . . .'

'Better you give your hero a close view of the tiger, so that he may flail and hug and tackle realistically. Has he seen the tiger?'

'Yes, from a distance – always from a distance, that's my problem. I notice that he shuts his eyes and trembles when he has to pass that cage! I was afraid how he would react to the tiger at close quarters . . .'

'How soon will your second unit arrive?'

'Within twenty-four hours.'

'No need to hurry,' said Captain. 'They may take three days. Meanwhile it is important that your giant and the tiger are introduced to each other; your artiste has to know what he is doing. As for Raja, as a general rule, it'll be good to give him a glimpse of his adversary.'

Madan was too preoccupied to question the logic of it or the need. It was one of the many routine remarks and suggestions that floated in the air during a film shooting and vanished. Madan summoned his assistant and instructed, 'Send a telegram to XL at Madras to dispatch the second unit within two days, one cameraman and a sound unit, and light unit . . .'

'Where is the need, sir,' asked the cameraman, overhearing the instruction while packing up, 'while you are not utilizing the first unit? What have we achieved the whole day?'

'None of your business to question. Be ready when you are asked,' Captain said sternly. Captain felt it was time to support Madan and establish his authority, and said, 'Shut your ears to our talk, understand? Open only when you are being addressed. In any event keep your mouth always shut, that'll help us all.' The cameraman was cowed by Captain's ringside manner and left, others trooping behind them.

From within his circle, where he had returned after the canteen visit, Jaggu cried, 'May I come out too?'

'Oh, poor fellow, they have forgotten you . . . Come.'

With a sigh of relief like a released animal Jaggu stepped out of his confinement of the Magic Circle. He was led into the make-up shed, and after a while came out without his costume, clad in a *lungi* and shirt with the paint off his face. There was relief in his face as he sat down on a bench to rest his legs after hours of standing. He lit a *beedi* and smoked it with contentment; he had eaten well at the canteen. One of Captain's circus hands who had escorted the tiger cage came up to him and said, 'Chief wants you to come . . .'

'Why?'

'To present you a cat . . .'

'Why a cat?' he asked with extreme innocence. The men who had come to summon him made a few merry jokes about a birthday gift and so forth. They led him through a gate into a stockade built for the cameraman, with platforms for taking top shots and enough gaps between the railings for the camera to follow the action in a larger enclosure. He saw a man with a whip in one hand and a chair in the other standing and commanding, 'Raja, come out.' The whip cracked and a tiger jumped out of its cage. 'Race round,' commanded the man. The tiger ran around, while Jaggu stood petrified, unable to believe his eyes.

Madan was watching him with attention and said, 'Fellow looks nervous but must get used to the idea even if we are faking the shot . . .' He watched the giant's discomfiture with glee. At one point the tiger lunged forward with a roar in Jaggu's direction and dashed against the stockade. Jaggu let out a howl, '*Amma*! Save me!' calling on his long-dead mother, and blindly smashed his way out.

Madan was saying to the Captain, 'This is a thing which you

might use in an emergency, but generally to tame any wild thing . . .' He produced a gadget, which when pressed shot out a thin metal rod, and at a touch delivered a shock, working on a battery. Madan explained, 'Only fifteen volts, but enough to keep any animal well behaved . . . You can try it if you like.'

'On Raja? Never, sir. My whip is enough.' He would not touch the gadget. He shook his head. 'I'd be ashamed to employ this on any animal. No trainer worth his name can be proud of it if his animal is coerced and beaten down with such a contraption. It's no training. It's stampeding an animal into obedience with electric shock . . .'

'Well, I don't know what you mean: you are doing it all the time.'

'If you don't see the difference, it's no use explaining further. I don't want short-cuts and hope that I do not destroy the natural pride an animal possesses . . . I'll take care of it.'

Although Madan could not admit that Captain actually practised all this theory, but was only letting his eloquence flow on, he just put away the gadget with, 'All I need is your cooperation.'

Of that word, he was very fond, as Captain noted with amusement; he repeated, 'Cooperation! Cooperation! That you can have in plenty, but not the tiger bullied and stunned with electric shocks . . .'

'Oh, come, come – it's not worse than the whip. In Hollywood they are using it all the time.'

'Probably even on the human stars, who may need to be kept awake!'

'I was for a moment lost in the fun of hearing "*Amma*" from this mountain of a baby. Where is he gone? Don't let him get away. Stun him if necessary,' said Madan, sending his men after Jaggu.

Captain could not help laughing at the huge character running away in panic, shouting for his mother's help. 'That fellow didn't even notice that he was in a different enclosure from the tiger – didn't notice the bars intervening. Didn't trust them, I suppose . . .'

Madan began to look concerned when his men did not turn up. 'Where could he have gone? Gone only five minutes . . . Where are the fellows who ran after him? They are also gone! Everyone seems to be too ready to desert us today . . .' He was rambling on irrelevantly in his anxiety and trying to put the blame on everyone.

Captain was apparently getting a lot of enjoyment out of it. 'If you had kept the camera on and shot this sequence of a giant running away at the sight of the tiger, it'd have been the greatest hit . . .'

'While all the time I want him to be heroic and tackle a tiger in keeping with his size!' Madan said ruefully.

Presently the searching party returned and reported: 'Nowhere.'

'What do you mean by it?' Madan asked angrily. 'He is not a tot to be lost sight of . . . can't be hiding behind a blade of grass.'

'We beat about every bush, every ditch and crag. We went up over a mile in three directions.'

'He must be found, otherwise I'll be ruined,' lamented Madan.

'Just take your car and try,' suggested Captain.

Madan started his car and drove down the road recklessly. 'If he is not found, I'll be ruined,' he kept saying to himself.

Madan was back within an hour with the giant stuffed like a baggage in the narrow back seat of his car, which had only two doors and could release a back-seat passenger only by folding down the front seat. It was like locking up a prisoner. Madan looked happy and relieved. 'I found him in old *Mari* shrine. Some instinct told me he must be there; other places could not conceal him.' He addressed Jaggu: 'The Goddess would not protect you. You know why? Because you tried to cheat me. Goddess doesn't like persons who try to cheat.'

'I don't like tigers,' Jaggu said.

'We don't care what you like or dislike,' Madan said. 'You are under contract with me. I told you the story before signing the agreement. If you act like a coward now, I will hand you over to the police.'

'But I didn't know it'd be a big tiger, it tried to kill me.'

'Didn't you see the bars between you and the tiger? We will see it doesn't touch you. You will be safe.'

Jaggu was on the point of tears. 'Leave me, sir, I am no good for this. Let me go back to my village. I'll display my strength and make my living.'

Madan was unmoved by all this pleading. 'They will have you in chains and put you to break stones . . .'

'I won't mind it, sir,' he said, habituated to breaking stones and chains for a living at all fairs. As a threat it misfired. While all this talk was going on, Madan hadn't yet released him from the back seat. The giant did not know how to come out of it. He said, 'Please, sir, let me out. My knees are paining, I can't sit here . . .' When that had no effect, he said, 'I've got to . . .' indicating he had to relieve himself.

Madan opened the door, pushed the seat forward, and hustled him out of the car. The giant got out and raced toward a bush. Madan shouted, 'If you try to trick me again, I'll release the tiger out of the cage and set him on you.' He directed two men to follow him. When he returned with the two bodyguards, Madan said, 'You must cooperate with me and I'll make you rich – a famous man. Your photo will be on all walls and papers . . . They will present their notebooks and beg you to sign . . .'

'No, sir, I was never taught how to read or write . . . If they had only put me to school I would have been different. I don't like tigers. Please save me . . .'

'You have signed or put your left thumb impression to an agreement in which you have agreed to act along with a tiger. But let me tell you, you will not be required to come close to the tiger. I will see that you are not hurt. Also remember the tiger is not all – it's only a part. I have written a story in which you knock down the tiger, kill it, and then marry a beautiful girl . . . I'm sure you will like it.'

He was horrified. 'Oh, no, I'm married . . . I'll go back to the village to give her money, whatever I earn . . .'

'All right, all right, you can take a lot of money for her.'

His bodyguards took him away at a signal from Madan and kept him company, enjoying a lot of jokes at his expense about bigamy. They led him away to a secluded spot on the location and said, 'Our boss has a beautiful bride for you . . . and yet you try to run away.'

Jaggu was horrified. 'Oh! I can't, my wife will –'

'Oh, your wife! Don't mind what she says. She is a country girl, but our boss has reserved for you a princess – oh, you will have to go through with it whether you like it or not. You have signed an agreement . . .'

'Don't you know that a film star should have at least two wives?'

'It is a government order,' said another.

'Our hut in the village is small . . .' Jaggu pleaded.

'You are going to be rich and can afford two houses for two wives.'

'You can sleep with one half the night, get up and go in a car to the other the other half of the night . . . Lucky fellow!'

'My wife will not like it . . . I don't want two wives.'

'Wait till you see the other one . . . You will save her from the tiger, and she'll call you her lord and saviour and darling for your trouble . . .'

Jaggu looked distressed and brooded over the terrible prospects that lay before him. He lit a *beedi* and thought over it. 'No, no,' he said to himself, 'I can't accept a tiger . . .'

'It's all written down like fate, nothing can be changed,' they taunted him.

He was rehearsed endlessly and made to go through the motions

[94]

of wrestling with an unseen tiger. Madan himself was fatigued demonstrating, out of the range of the camera, the gestures, which the giant had to copy while the camera was shooting. Though the hero was the only one in the cast for the present sequence, the film personnel of two units created quite a crowd, and were all over the place.

At the other end of the lot Captain was handling Raja. He had extended the time for shooting by several weeks, since Madan had agreed to pay heavily for the extension, and Captain felt it was a sound way of making money during the interval between two camps. Although he was indifferent generally in money matters, now a certain degree of greed was overcoming him, a gradual corruption through contact with the film world. He began to think, 'What a lot of money this film business turns over. Let me collect the loot, while this fool of a Madan is about it.' He told his wife, 'Possibly after this, Madan may come up with an idea for making a full circus-picture, that'll be a good break for us . . .'

She welcomed the idea. 'Don't discourage him. "Cooperate" with that fellow, as he always says. If he wants more days for shooting, grant it . . . We could always delay the opening of the next camp. Anyway I'm tired and bored with the circus. Let us try something new for a change. We lose nothing. We may be free from all this dust and noise and ticket-selling for some time.'

'We have to depend upon Raja now too much, and beg him to "cooperate", but his act is rather difficult. He is required to stand on his hind legs and fall forward. Every day I'm trying to make him understand, but it's proving difficult . . .'

'Why don't you try the electrical gadget?'

'I won't hear of it. Impossible.'

At this point their pleasantries came to an end and she castigated him for being impractical and sentimental. 'After all he'll be limp for a few minutes, when you can manoeuvre him for the camera. I'm prepared to handle your Raja with the electric staff if you lack the guts. I am confident I can manage. Give me two men, Sam and the other fellow – what's his name? Muniswami . . .'

'Very well,' Captain said, 'I'll keep away tomorrow, you try . . .'

'I mean it,' she said.

'You mind your business,' he said. 'Tumble on your trapeze and read a novel if you can't spend your time. If you feel dull without work, why don't you spend a week at Lovedale, visiting the boys?'

'So that you may breathe freely? You always find my presence irksome!'

'Not always but sometimes. Whatever you want to do, keep off my animals. They won't obey you because you are my wife.'

'Ah, ah, you are modest, aren't you?'

I did not like it in the least. Day after day I had to do the same thing over and over again. Captain came up at the same hour. The whip and the chair were back in use. A motley crowd around, outside the enclosure, watching me perform acts which I never understood. In the circus ring also there would be many men, but they all helped the show, carried out Captain's orders, brought in whatever was required for the show, and took it away after the act. They moved slowly and never spoke much. But here were men who were ordering each other all the time. A man at the camera was commanding everybody, shouting at the top of his voice all the time, 'More left, no not so much, go back, light . . .' When he said 'light', a blinding radiance would appear. I missed all the good things I had got used to in the circus. There one performed one's duties and quickly went back home. The band music, and the men and women seated around in chairs, and their voices and the lights were very welcome and became a part of one's life. But here, outside the ring, they behaved as if they were seized with fever . . .

The cameraman ordered even Captain. He was constantly telling him to shift and move: 'Captain, if you want the tiger alone in the shot, you should step back, and manoeuvre the tiger from out of range.' Captain became submissive. It was unbelievable that he should be taking orders from others; I could not understand what had happened to him. He would crack his whip and get me out of the cage, and order, 'Up, up' every time and hit my legs till I lifted them; gradually he compelled me to tilt back and rise – a terrible trial for me and very painful, and I always fell back or forward, and went on bruising myself. And all the time the cameraman went on bawling out something or the other and shooting from his protected shelter. He was never satisfied and wanted me to repeat, improve, further improve and repeat, my Captain blindly carrying out his orders, whipping, hitting and yelling. This went on day after day. They neither gave me rest nor showed kindness – Captain was losing grip over himself and his self-respect. Often Madan came to watch, gave his own directions along with the cameraman. Between the two they seemed to have enslaved Captain. All the polished gentleness Madan had displayed till now was gone. He was gradually gaining the upper hand, often spoke of the money he had thrown away, and of his enterprise as a blunder. Captain was still calm. He said, 'Don't talk nonsense. This is an extremely intelligent tiger, but you demand impossible actions from him.'

'I only expect what you yourself suggested at our discussion. I never thought a man of your calibre would suggest impossible things . . .' Thus went on their talks. Soon they devised a method to stand me on my hind legs. When Captain brought me out of the cage, I found dangled before me a lamb. As I reached out, the lamb rose in the air gradually. I was interested now, and tried to reach it; it went up so slowly that I had to stand up and try to keep my balance, and then it would go out of my reach up and up, and no amount of straining on my part would help – even though I stretched myself fully and stood up like a human being and fell forward. A creature needs the support of four legs for stability. Somehow human beings balance on two legs . . . It's not only difficult but a degradation for a quadruped – you are too exposed;

no wonder humans have to cover their waists. While they tempted me with a bait to stand up, the camera followed my action, the act repeated till I was sick of it. Monotonous and tedious it was. Morning till night and sometimes with blinding lights at night.

I became desperate. Once at the start of the day, I refused to take note of the lamb dangling before me. I looked at him and looked away indifferently, but Captain would not let me be. If I had had the gift of speech, I'd have said, 'Please leave me out of it today, I'm worn out.' But I could only growl and roar. Not all his whipping and yelling could move me out of the cage. But now a thing happened which I had never experienced before. He tucked his whip under his arm and brought out a novel object, which shot out a tongue of metal; at its touch I felt blinded with a strange kind of pain and helplessness, and ran out of the cage. Anything to escape the touch of that vicious tongue. I just collapsed on the ground outside the cage, my legs aching with all that jumping to catch the dangling lamb of the previous day.

But Captain would not let me lie down. The cameraman and Madan were shouting, 'Get him on his legs, the reel is running out. Come on . . .' Captain lashed me in the face, and then quietened down; 'Come on, be a good boy. You can rest tomorrow,' in the gentlest tone as always between two lashings. When it didn't move me, he assumed a third pitch of voice, which could reach the skies, and hit me on the nose, which would usually drive me to obedience. Today it only stirred my anger. I swished my tail and grunted. He knew what it meant, that I'd not be easy to handle. But he was not the one to care for my inclinations. It was his will that counted, he knew he could finally impose it on me. I shuddered at the idea of going after that elusive lamb again. If I could have spoken, I would have told him, 'Go away before any harm befalls you, my good man. After all you have fed me and protected me. I shall honour you for it. But please go away and leave me alone. I won't be your slave any more, I'll never go back to my cage; that's all, I won't do

[98]

any of the meaningless turns these foolish men around want me to do. It was different at the circus, but the present activities appear to me senseless and degrading. I won't go through them. I like this air and freedom. I'm not going to give it up now. Later perhaps, when you have regained your judgement, I'll return to your circus, but please don't drive me back to the cage now. Please understand and leave me alone. Please listen to my advice.'

But he was a stubborn fellow with no doubt whatever about his own notions. He brought his whip down on my nose again, at a point where it hurt most. I let out a roar, involuntarily, stung by it. That made him more angry. He took it as a piece of impudence on my part. He brought his whip again in quick succession over my eyes indiscriminately. I wanted to scream loudly, 'Oh, Captain, don't be foolhardy, your life is in danger, go away, leave me before any calamity befalls you.' But he was drunk with authority. I wished he could save himself, but he was not helping himself at all. He would not rest till he exacted total submission. I noticed him tucking the whip under his arm and slipping his free hand in his pocket to bring out the dreadful instrument which would shoot out a metal tongue. He'd only touch me, as with a feather, to make me dizzy and servile.

I caught myself thinking, 'Why should I fear this creature no bigger than my tail?' First time in my life such an idea was occurring. So far I had never measured him. But today he looked puny to me in spite of all his yelling and angry gestures. In recognition of our relationship and as a final warning I growled and just raised my paw. He cried, 'Ah! ah! – you threaten me!' and forgetting himself enough to approach me beyond the margin of safety which he always maintained for an emergency retreat, he dashed forward with that vicious metal tongue shooting out of its sheath. As he stooped down to caress me with its tip, I just raised a forepaw, taking care to retract my claws, and knocked the thing out of his hand. The blow caught Captain under his chin, and tore off his head. It was surprising that such a flimsy creature, no better than a membrane stretched over some thin framework, with so little stuff inside, should have held me in fear so long.

Much confusion and excitement and running. I got up to move freely for the first time. The crew at first tried to save their equipment in the pandemonium, but abandoned it and fled. I heard Madan say, 'I'm ruined, mind the cables, don't trip over. You'll bring down the lights.' Lights or something did come crashing; the cameraman disappeared.

When I had moved off some distance from the cage, the giant, who had been in action, suddenly made a dash into the cage I had vacated and pulled down the door. A number of others battered on the door, but filling all the space he would not take anyone in. Madan's voice could be heard over the uproar: 'Who has the gun? Where is the fellow in charge of it? Absurd situation . . .' No one had the calmness to answer any question: each was looking to his own safety and escape, while I calmly walked off the lot. The cameraman had abandoned his camera on its stand; while moving away, I brushed against it and sent it toppling down with a bang. Some unseen man was crying, 'The zoom is gone. Ruined, ruined . . .'

It was still a busy hour in the city when I entered Market Road. People ran for their lives at the sight of me. As I progressed through, shutters were pulled down, and people hid themselves under culverts, on trees, behind pillars. The population was melting out of sight. At the circus I had had no chance to study human behaviour. Outside the circus ring they sat in their seats placidly while I cowered before Captain's whip. I got a totally wrong notion of human beings at that angle. I had thought that they were sturdy and fearless. But now I found them fleeing before me like a herd of deer, although I had no intention of attacking them. When I paused in front of a tailor's shop, he abandoned his machine and shut himself in a cupboard, wailing, 'Alas, I am undone, won't someone shoot that tiger?' A prisoner between two constables, who had been caught for murder and was just emerging from the Court House, got his chance to escape when the constables fled, abandoning him with his handcuffs. I tore a horse from its *jutka* and enjoyed the sight of the passengers spilling out of it and running for their lives. A couple of street dogs invited destruction when they barked madly, instead of minding their business.

Later, I learnt from my Master of the chaos that befell the city when it became known that Captain had been destroyed and that I was somewhere in the city. Sheer hopelessness seems to have seized the townspeople. They withdrew to their homes and even there remained nervous. All doors and windows everywhere were shut, bolted, and sealed. Some even thought that I was some extraordinary creature who might pass through the walls and lie in wait on the roof or in the loft or basement. Poor people living in huts had real cause to worry: I could have taken any of their homes apart. But why should I? One could understand their fears, but why should those living in brick and cement feel nervous? It was due to their general lack of a sense of security and an irrational dread of losing their assets. Why should an ordinary simple tiger have any interest in them either to destroy or to safeguard?

I rested for a moment at the door of Anand Bhavan, on Market Road, where coffee drinkers and tiffin eaters at their tables sat transfixed, uttering low moans on seeing me. I wanted to assure them, 'Don't fear, I am not out to trouble you. Eat your tiffin in peace, don't mind me ... You, nearest to me, hugging the cash box, you are craven with fear, afraid even to breathe. Go on, count the cash, if that's your pleasure. I just want to watch, that's all ... If my tail trails down to the street, if I am blocking your threshold, it is because, I'm told, I'm eleven feet tip to tail. I can't help it. I'm not out to kill ... I'm too full – found a green pasture teeming with food on the way. Won't need any for several days to come, won't stir, not until I feel hungry again. Tigers attack only when they feel hungry, unlike human beings who slaughter one another without purpose or hunger . . .'

To the great delight of children, schools were being hurriedly closed. Children of all ages and sizes were running helter-skelter, screaming joyously, 'No school, no school. Tiger, tiger!' They were shouting and laughing and even enjoyed being scared. They seemed to welcome me. I felt like joining them, and bounded away from the restaurant door and trotted along with them, at which they gleefully cried, 'The tiger is coming to eat us; let us get back to the school!'

I followed them through their school gate while they ran up and shut themselves in the school hall securely. I ascended the steps of the school, saw an open door at the far end of a veranda, and walked in. It happened to be the headmaster's room, I believed, as I noticed a very dignified man jumping on his table and heaving himself up into an attic. I walked in and flung myself on the cool floor, having a partiality for cool stone floor, with my head under the large desk – which gave me the feeling of being back in the Mempi cave . . . As I drowsed, I was aware of cautious steps and hushed voices all around. I was in no mood to bother about anything. All I wanted was a little moment of sleep; the daylight was dazzling. In half sleep I heard the doors of the room being shut and bolted and locked. I didn't care. I slept.

While I slept a great deal of consultation was going on. I learnt about it later through my Master, who was in the crowd – the crowd which had gathered after making sure that I had been properly locked up – and was watching. The headmaster seems to have remarked some days later, 'Never dreamt in my wildest mood that I'd have to yield my place to a tiger . . .' A wag had retorted, 'Might be one way of maintaining better discipline among the boys.'

'Now that this brute is safely locked up, we must decide –' began a teacher.

At this moment my Master pushed his way through the crowds and admonished, 'Never use the words *beast* or *brute*. They're ugly words coined by man in his arrogance. The human being thinks all other creatures are "beasts". Awful word!'

'Is this the occasion to discuss problems of vocabulary?' asked someone.

'Why not?' retorted my Master. At which they looked outraged.

Someone said, 'What a reckless man you are! Who are you?'

'You are asking a profound question. I've no idea who I am! All my life I have been trying to find the answer. Are you sure you know who you are?'

'Crazy beggar – with a tiger in there ready to devour us, but for the strong door . . . There is no time for useless talk. Let us get on with the business . . .'

'What business? What is it going to be?' asked my Master.

Everyone was upset at this question. 'We must think of those children shut in the hall,' said a teacher.

'Open the door and let them out,' said my Master, unasked.

'Not your business to advise us; who are you?'

'Second time you are asking the same question. I say again, I don't know,' said my Master.

'Get out of the school premises,' said a man who acted for the headmaster in his absence. 'You have no business here. We can't have all kinds of intruders . . .'

'Did the tiger come on your invitation?' asked my Master.

'We have to think seriously what to do now. Please leave us alone. Go away, I say,' commanded the acting headmaster.

At which my Master said, 'A headmaster must be obeyed in his school, even if he is only acting,' and slipped back to the farthest end of the veranda.

'Go away,' they all shouted.

'I'll stay, but promise not to disturb your consultations . . .' And then my Master withdrew to a far corner to watch them, to observe how they were going to tackle the tiger. They constantly turned their heads and threw furtive looks at him, feeling uneasy to talk in his presence, but at the same time finding it difficult to order him out. They lowered their voices. The acting headmaster said, 'Now we have to decide on the next step to take . . .'

'Yes, yes,' chorused his assistant masters.

'We must get someone to shoot it. Who has a gun in our town?'

Everyone fell into deep thinking. The mathematics teacher, the most practical-minded in the institution, said, 'I'm sure the police will have it. Send someone to fetch the superintendent.'

I must have turned in my sleep and knocked over some piece of furniture and that seemed to have scared them further. All of them cried, 'Let us go, it is perhaps trying to break open the door!' and started to retreat desperately.

At this point my Master shouted from his corner, 'He can't open the door. He has no hands. Only some furniture . . .'

Whereupon they glared at him and said, 'If you are going to be here, take care not to interrupt our talks.'

My Master, being calm and wise, merely said, 'Very well, I won't interrupt.'

The mathematics teacher now said, 'Shall I call the police to handle the tiger?'

Another teacher had a misgiving at this point: 'I doubt if this is a police matter. No law has been broken . . .'

'Is it lawful to let loose a tiger in a public thoroughfare?'

'Who let it loose? No one. It came by itself.'

'The circus man is responsible.'

'But he is dead . . . They must arrest the film producer for endangering public safety.'

'Where are they? They have all vanished – fled before the tiger . . . took their shattered cameras too . . . We can't go after them now.

I wouldn't be surprised if the tiger has swallowed them up...'

'I wouldn't think so,' said my Master again. 'He is not a man-eater...'

'Isn't he? Have you tested him?' asked the acting headmaster, rather viciously, annoyed at the fact that the man was still there.

My Master said, 'I don't notice any progress in your talk. Why don't you let all the children go home without making any noise ... and all of you may also go home...'

'And leave the tiger in charge of the school?' asked the acting headmaster with an untimely irony. And added, 'You must go. We don't want you on the premises, whatever we may decide...' said the acting headmaster, glaring at my Master.

At which my Master shouted back, 'If my presence is the real problem rather than the tiger, I'll go, but you will see me again, I have no doubt,' rather mysteriously and went off. All eyes followed him till he disappeared beyond the school gate. My Master was only out of their vision, but was at hand, sitting on a culvert keenly watching the goings-on at the school veranda, not missing a single word of their confused babble. He heard, 'Get a gun immediately.'

'Does anyone know how to shoot?'

'The Superintendent of Police has a gun...'

'But he can't use it unless a magistrate orders...'

'Where does he live? He used to be in the New Extension ... that yellow house in the Third Cross corner.'

'Now he has moved to the government quarters...'

'Better we get Alphonse. He is a good *shikari*, licensed double-barrelled gun. The walls of his house are covered with bison heads and stuff like that. He's a good shot.'

'But he is a declared poacher; they have confiscated his gun.'

'Can't be, I saw him yesterday at Market Gate...'

'Did you see him with a gun?'

'Why should he take his gun to the market? I spoke to him and he said he was going to camp in the forest the next four days –'

'It is rumoured that they have taken away his hunting licence . . .'

'But he said he was shooting with a camera.'

'His camera may shoot bullets, too. Don't you believe such fellows – they are really poachers.'

Now I let out a growl, a mild one, and that brought their minds back to the business on hand.

'Better get the D.F.O.'

'What is D.F.O.?'

'You mean you don't know D.F.O. means District Forest Officer?' At which the man thus corrected was annoyed, and insults and angry words were exchanged until the acting headmaster intervened and reminded them that they were engaging themselves in an untimely wasteful talk. And then he turned to the school servant to ask, 'Do you know where the D.F.O. lives?'

'No, sir,' he said promptly.

A student came forward – a young fellow who had managed to stay back when all others had rushed into the school hall. 'Ravi is my friend, I know where he lives.'

'Who is Ravi?' His answer was drowned in a lot of cross-talk.

'Don't forget the H.M. can't come down. How long can he be crouching in that loft?'

'How are you sure that he climbed into the loft?'

'They had a glimpse while shutting the door . . . Don't waste time in this sort of cross-examination.'

They seemed to be incapable of reaching any practical solution. My Master, who had been sitting on the culvert, came back to say, 'If you keep chatting like this, I'll dash up and let the tiger out . . .'

'Oh, would you? You will be the first fellow to be devoured,' said an idiot. And all the members said, 'We said you should keep out of here, why have you come back?'

'Just to see if you fellows will do or say anything useful. Pity the children whose education and training are in your hands . . .'

At which the acting headmaster drew himself up to say, 'Get out of this place, this is our school. In the absence of the headmaster, I take his place automatically. I have told you that already.'

'Yes, yes, I remember; I have also said that when a headmaster, even if he is only acting, gives an order, it must be obeyed instantly,' and he went back to his seat on the culvert at the gate, beyond their range of vision but not out of earshot.

Presently he saw a man arrive on a noisy motor cycle, drowning all other sound, carrying a gun. He slowed down near my Master to ask excitedly, 'I heard of a tiger being somewhere here – is it true?'

My Master indicated the school, but added, 'You can't shoot him, if that's your idea . . .' Ignoring it, the man turned into the gate with a haughty toss of his head.

Now my Master followed a fresh motley crowd drifting in, driven by a mixture of curiosity and fear. Now that they knew the tiger was locked up, throngs of men and women were in the streets purposelessly wandering and vaguely looking for the tiger. All normal activity in the city was suspended. In the crowd one could find lawyers in their black gowns, shopmen who had pulled down the shutters, hawkers with trays on their heads, policemen in uniform, and so forth. The school had never seen such a crowd before in its compound and veranda. An army of anxious parents arrived, desperately searching for their children. They dashed hither and thither and towards the headmaster's room in a body, demanding, 'Where are our children? We want our children safely back. What sort of a school that they can't protect our children when a tiger is about?'

A teacher was provoked by this remark. 'Why do you presume such things? Haven't we a responsibility?'

'Where are our children? My child is only seven years old.

It's a mistake to have sent him to this wretched tiger-infested school.'

'You perhaps are always ready to attack the school . . .'

A burly parent came up shaking his fist. 'Don't go on philosophizing. We don't want your philosophy. Where are the children? You should have closed the school when the tiger was known to have escaped into the town. If anything happens to the child, I'll smash you all and set fire to the school.'

The teacher looked scared between a bully and the tiger. He said in a trembling voice, 'We let them off early, but they came back.'

Meanwhile a group, having heard the shouts of the children locked up in the hall, went up and forced open the door, and the children poured out of the room like flood water released from a sluice, screaming and roaring with joy. Confusion was at its maximum.

The man with the gun strode in with the gun in position, shouting at the top of his voice: 'Keep away, everybody. I won't be responsible if anyone is hurt. I'll count. Before I count ten, everyone must clear out of the way. Otherwise I shoot and won't be responsible for any mishap to any individual,' and he held up and flourished his double-barrelled gun, asking, 'Is he in there? I can shoot through the door . . .'

'Oh, no, don't. The headmaster is also in there.'

'He went up into the loft and is crouching there . . .'

'I'll aim and hit right on it, only the tiger. You may keep a flower on its back or even the headmaster himself, but my bullet will leave everything else untouched and bring down the beast alone.'

At this moment my Master came forward to say, 'Never use that word again . . .'

'Which word?' asked Alphonse the gunman.

' "Beast" is an ugly, uncharitable expression.'

'Mind your business.'

'This is my business,' answered my Master, and people, fearing that he might be shot, pulled him away. The gunman continued his plans.

'But how are you to know where he is in that room?'

'If the door is pushed open slightly, I can immediately –'

'If the tiger dashes out?'

'Oh, a moving target is no problem. I have brought down creatures running at one hundred miles an hour . . .'

'No, no, opening the door is out of the question, impossible.'

'Get me a ladder, then. I'll go up and shoot from the roof . . . enough if a couple of tiles are removed . . .' Someone was hustled to fetch a ladder from a neighbouring house. They all waited in silence. Somehow the sight of the gunman seemed to have subdued the crowd. They spoke in hushed voices. 'Where is the ladder?' demanded Alphonse. 'Who is gone to fetch one?' he asked with an air of command. People looked at each other, and no one came up with an answer. At which Alphonse stamped his foot like a spoilt child, and demanded angrily, 'Who is in charge here?' The acting headmaster was unwilling to come forward now, with the tiger on one side and the gun-wielder on the other. He had tried to make himself obscure and slip away unnoticed. But others seized him by his arm and propelled him forward, crying, 'Here is the First Assistant, he is in charge when the headmaster is away.'

The acting headmaster said, 'The H.M. is still there in his room. He is not away actually.'

'Oh, oh,' someone jeered.

'But is he in a position to issue orders?'

'Perhaps not – may not be audible if he talks from inside the tiger,' a wag suggested. And there was giggling all round.

At this my Master came forward to ask, 'Is this the time for levity?'

Alphonse turned on him fiercely. 'Who are you?'

My Master said, 'Oh, once again the same question! I wish I could answer with so many asking the same question.'

'I am not prepared to waste time talking to you . . . Now be off. Don't interrupt, I don't care who you are or what you are . . . you loincloth-covered, bearded loon . . .' He then turned his attention to the acting headmaster and asked sternly, 'Are you in charge of this school?'

'Yes, only when the headmaster is on leave. Not when he is in there . . .' He pointed at the headmaster's room.

Alphonse glared at him and said, 'I know you are trying to be slippery. Heaven help you if you are going to be tricky. I like people to be straightforward and truthful . . . You are the man in charge. If you think you are going to have your chance to take his place by letting him be eaten up, you are mistaken. I am determined to get him out intact – if I have to shoot down everything in my way, I'll do it. Now get me a ladder. It's urgent.' The acting headmaster was speechless; the crowed watched in a state of hushed awe. Some persons were trying to leave, unable to judge how the situation might develop and anticipating bloodshed. Alphonse held the acting headmaster with his look and demanded, 'Get me a ladder at once.'

'We have no ladder in this school,' he said timidly.

'Do you mean to say,' Alphonse asked contemptuously, 'that you run a school like this without a ladder?'

'What is a ladder for in a teaching institution?' questioned the assistant headmaster in a foolhardy manner.

'Don't be impudent,' said Alphonse, glaring at him, at which the assistant headmaster took fright and tried to mollify him by saying, 'Headmaster requisitioned for one last year, but the D.P.I.'s office are holding up the sanction. Unless they sanction the budget, we can't even buy a pin . . .'

'The procedure is silly,' commented Alphonse.

A few others murmured, 'True, sir, we all agree with you. We can't buy even a cane except through the D.P.I.'s sanction.'

'What do you want a cane for?' demanded Alphonse, going off

at a tangent. 'Do you mean to say you are using it on the boys? Whenever I find teachers doing that, I give them a taste of it first . . .'

'Oh, no, I just mentioned cane because it came to my mind. We never do such things . . . We get cattle straying into our garden and we use the stick to drive them away.'

'Hmm . . . you had better be careful. If you teachers wish to save your skins, remember I'll as readily bag wild pedagogues as I do wild animals of the forest.'

'Educational norms are different today.'

'What do you mean by it?' Alphonse asked severely, turning to the speaker.

'We have to handle them psychologically . . .'

'Good for you, keep it in mind.'

At this point two boys came through carrying a bamboo ladder between them and placed it before the crowd. Alphonse was delighted. He patted the boys' heads by turn, one by one, methodically. 'Where have you got this from?' he asked, very pleased.

'We ran to a house in Kabir Lane, I had noticed that they had kept a ladder in their back-yard, to pluck drumsticks from the tree, and now they had locked themselves in and also shut all the windows because of the tiger, and so I brought it away quietly and they did not see us. I was dragging it along, but Ramu saw me on the way and helped me and both of us carried it down – because we heard you asking for a ladder, I ran out at once, remembering the ladder in the next house . . .'

'You are a very intelligent, observant fellow. What is your name?'

'Shekar,' he answered proudly and loudly.

'Shekar,' cried Alphonse enthusiastically. 'Come and see me with your friend. I'll have a present for you. I've a wonderful air-gun, with which you can practise. You won't need a licence for it although you can hit and disable a buck at forty feet . . .

Our country needs more boys of your type. You are our only hope.'

'He is the brightest fellow in our school,' the assistant headmaster ventured to suggest with some pride, to please the gunman.

'I'm glad you recognize it, if you really mean it. Shekar, you and your friend take the ladder over there and put it up for me to go up to the roof . . .'

One couldn't have secured more spirited helpers. Shekar and Ramu felt so flattered that they were prepared to obey any command from Uncle Alphonse. 'He has promised me a gun. I'll shoot all the crows and dogs in our street.'

'I'll shoot the donkeys,' said Ramu.

'How can you?' Shekar asked. 'He has only one gun and that is promised to me.'

'It's for both of us,' Ramu said. 'Let us share it.'

'How can two shoot with a single gun?' sneered Shekar, but before it could develop into a full-scale argument, Alphonse cried, 'Come on, boys, march on with the ladder.'

The two boys took the ladder out to the spot indicated, and Alphonse placed it below the eaves of the headmaster's office. He then turned to a small crowd, which followed him. He braced himself for the task, put one foot on the first rung, and turned to face his audience: 'You must all be calm and mind your business if you have any. Don't get panicky if you hear gunshots presently. I can shoot straight and finally, of course, but there can be no guarantee how the tiger will behave when he is hit. Before I send the second shot and dispatch him, he may go mad and devilish and storm his way out of the room, he may spring skyward, or dash through the door or break the walls in his fury. One can't foresee what'll happen then, especially when I have not seen the brute –'

'He is no brute,' shouted my Master from back of the crowd. 'No more than any of us here.'

'Ah, ah! You are still here. You were ordered to remain out of range, weren't you? Anyway if you are still here you will see who is a brute when he comes out. However, if you have no business here, get out of this place smartly . . . I want two men up here to come up with me and loosen the tiles. If I see clearly inside, I can finish the job in a moment.'

'What about the headmaster, who must be somewhere between your gun and the animal?'

'That's a problem,' said Alphonse generously, 'but if you have confidence in me, he'll escape the shot.'

'But the tiger may spring up, you said, and God knows where he will be caught,' said someone.

Alphonse said, 'Don't imagine troubles. Have you confidence in me or not?' He paused and waited for an answer. It was Shekar who shouted at the top of his voice, 'Don't let them stop you, Uncle, go on and shoot the animal. I'd love to see how you shoot.'

'Follow me then and help to remove the tiles. I'll tell you how to do it . . . The grown-ups here are all cowards and ought to wear *saris*; they are afraid to see a tiger even from a rooftop.'

'I'm not afraid,' said Shekar, and his friend added a confirmation. Alphonse climbed the ladder, followed by the two boys, who were cautioned and admonished by their teachers for their fool-hardiness.

'If I had four arms like some of your gods,' said Alphonse from the roof, 'I would not have needed the help of these young people. Two of my hands would have pulled the tiles out, while the other two might have been holding the gun and triggering off the shot. Four arms are a most sensible arrangement.' And then he proceeded to remove a few tiles and asked the boys to follow his example. They tore up the tiles with zest and threw them down recklessly, enjoying the sight of their elders dodging below.

Soon an opening was made, and a shaft of sunlight entered the room. The headmaster was on the point of collapse, crouching there in the narrow attic, amidst bundles of old papers and files.

He looked up and saw the faces of the two boys on the roof and could not make out what they were doing up there. He could not believe his eyes. He tried to stand up, but hit his head on the rafters. Shekar cried, 'It's me, sir. My friend is also here, Ramu of Four B. Uncle is here to shoot the tiger . . .' The headmaster had enough wits about him to understand the situation. 'Sir, aren't you hungry? If you come out, I'll run up to Pankaja Cafe and bring you tiffin, if someone gives me money . . .' said the boy.

The headmaster took his finger to his lips to warn the boy not to make a noise and wake up the tiger. He spoke in a hoarse whisper. At the mention of the tiger, Shekar was pushed aside and in his place the headmaster found another head. 'I'm Alphonse,' said the man. 'Headmaster, keep cool; we will get you out soon. Ah! I see him there . . . must be eleven-point-five feet . . . a full-grown brute. Wish his head were not under the table. I could dispatch him with one shot then and there. You need have no doubt . . . I could shoot now, but if he is hit in the hind part, he may go mad and spring up. I've seen such beasts go up even fifteen feet in the air under similar circumstances. But first let me get you out of here . . . Keep cool . . . don't fall off the attic.' He looked around. 'Boy, you must run and get a hacksaw or an ordinary carpenter's saw. Run and get it as smartly as you brought the ladder. If you see a carpenter, snatch it from his bag.'

'Yes, you will need more than a carpenter's saw,' said a voice, and turning round Alphonse exclaimed, 'You, here still!'

'Yes, yes,' said my Master. 'I could come up a ladder as well as anyone.'

'Weren't you told to keep out?' asked Alphonse angrily.

'Yes, yes,' agreed my Master amiably, and added, 'Who are you to pass such orders?'

'You are a pertinacious pest,' remarked Alphonse in disgust. 'Now the urgent thing is that you get the saw. You stick like the

burr, but at least make yourself useful . . . go and get a saw immediately.'

'What for?'

Alphonse suppressed his irritation, and said, 'I want to saw off a
couple of those crossbars, enough to admit the headmaster's head,
and then we could pull him out and tackle the tiger.'

'And you expect the tiger to watch the fun while you are at your
carpentry?' Master said with a smile.

Alphonse said, 'If you do not behave, I'll push you in through
this gap. Shekar, get a saw without delay – instead of listening
to this mad fellow. He is persistent . . . No way of keeping him
off.'

'How can you keep me off? Who are you?' asked my Master,
and added, 'I can ask the same question you asked, who are you? I
know enough law to realize that I have as good a right to be on a
roof as anyone else!'

'I'm only here to help the headmaster . . .'

'You won't be able to work through the rafters so easily. They
are old teak beams. You will have to saw for days before you can
make a dent . . .'

'In that case, I'll shoot. I've enough sight now. Let the headmaster
stay where he is, and take his chance and pray for his life and pray
that the tiger does not spring up vertically . . .' He turned to the
headmaster, who was peering out like a prisoner behind the bars:
'Only be careful that you don't fall off the edge when you hear my
gun go off, stick close to the wall so that even if the tiger springs
up, you will stay clear of his reach. With the second, I'll get him,
even if he is in mid air . . .'

'Oh, here they are,' exclaimed my Master, pointing at the school
gate. A jeep had arrived at the gate and a number of persons
jumped out of it and hurried across the school compound. They
pushed their way through the crowd.

'Come down, please, and keep your finger off the trigger. We are

[115]

Save Tiger Committee. You must hear us first. We are a statutory body with police powers . . .'

Alphonse came down the ladder, saying, 'The headmaster is about to be saved. Please give me five minutes, I'll get him out and then we can discuss.'

The wild-life committee paused to consider it for a moment, and asked, 'Explain how you propose to save the headmaster.'

Alphonse explained that he proposed to cut through the rafters and bail out the headmaster.

My Master, who had followed him down, said, 'Rafters are of ancient timber, it'll take at least three days to make a notch.'

Alphonse glared at him and exclaimed, 'You again! Why do you dog my steps like this? I'd knock you down with the butt, but for your age. The animal is there already stirring and growling. How long do you think the headmaster will stand the tension? He may faint and roll off the attic straight into the mouth of the tiger. You won't let me call him a beast. I don't know why I'm being plagued by you . . . you follow me like a shadow . . .'

My Master ignored Alphonse and turned to the visitors: 'I'm grateful that you have responded to my call. If you hadn't come, he'd have murdered the tiger. His plan was to make enough noise with a saw or anything to stir up the animal, and shoot, leaving it to chance for the headmaster to survive . . .'

Alphonse ground his teeth and remained silent. Meanwhile Shekar plucked at his sleeve. 'Uncle, give me money, I'll buy *idli* and *vadai* at the Pankaja restaurant for the headmaster . . .' Alphonse fished out of his pocket a rupee and gave it to the boy, who at once ran off. Alphonse said, looking after him, 'This fellow is the hope of our country. He is fit to ride on the back of a tiger . . .'

The leader of the wild-life group said, 'Mr Alphonse, as you may be aware, I'm the chairman of the local chapter of Tiger Project, affiliated to the Central Committee under the Ministry of Agriculture at Delhi . . .'

[116]

'What has agriculture to do with tigers?' asked Alphonse.

'We will go into the question later, but at the moment we wish to emphasize the fact that "Save Tiger Project", as its name indicates, is to prevent the decimation of the tiger population which was at one time in the neighbourhood of fifteen thousand; today it's less than fifteen hundred.' He went into statistics until Alphonse said, 'Is this the time for a lecture, while the headmaster is half dead inside? You think that only tigers are important and not a headmaster . . .'

'And so,' continued the chairman, 'there is a general ordinance issued by the government which prohibits the shooting of any tiger, in any part of India, and we are given powers to enforce the rules and initiate prosecution if and when necessary; with penalty up to two thousand rupees and one year's rigorous imprisonment and confiscation of the offender's weapon and licence . . .'

'I know all this and more,' said Alphonse. 'You are opening your eyes on this subject probably only now. But I have been in the tiger business for half a century. There's a provision in the same ordinance, an exemption where a man-eater is concerned . . .'

'Yes, yes, we know all that; where a tiger has been established to be a man-eater, we can permit the shooting, provided you apply for it with proof and evidence . . .'

'What proof? Remains of a poor villager snatched away from the tiger's jaw? I'll also have to file a photograph and write an application in triplicate, I suppose?' he asked, with grim humour. 'You and your government regulations. You have no practical sense . . . You'll see half the population destroyed in your zeal to protect the tiger: perhaps that's a ruse to keep down the population of our country! Ha! Ha! Ha! Here's a headmaster struggling to survive and you go on talking rules. You people do not distinguish between what's important and unimportant.'

Meanwhile I awoke after a very good stretch of sleep and heard voices outside. I looked up and saw the headmaster cowering in the attic. I stretched myself and roared, for no particular reason except that I felt alive. The poor human being in the loft must have trembled at that moment. I wished to assure him that I was not going to hurt him. If it had been the old jungle days, I'd have gone after him; already a change was coming over me, I think. My Master's presence in the vicinity, though he had not come near me yet, must have begun to affect me. I tried to assure the headmaster by raising myself and putting up my forelegs on the wall and scratching it, and growling softly, which must have shaken the poor man so much that he seemed to lose control of his bowels and bladder. Thereupon I withdrew from the wall and curled myself under the table once again in order to reassure the poor man . . .

Meanwhile, outside, my Master noticed Alphonse taking the chairman aside under a tree, where they spoke in whispers. When they came back, the chairman was a changed man. He took aside, in his turn, his committee members, and spoke to them. Thereupon they took papers out of a briefcase and signed and gave them to Alphonse. All this concerned me. I was declared a man-eater and Alphonse was given written permission to shoot. 'In the normal course,' explained the chairman, 'I should get the sanction from Delhi, but in an emergency, I am empowered to use my discretion.' My Master suspected that Alphonse had offered a substantial bribe, as he was known to be engaged in a flourishing business exporting tiger skins.

Shekar was seen coming down the ladder with a packet of food in hand. He approached Alphonse. 'Uncle, I can't see the headmaster; I held out the *idli*, but he didn't take it. What shall I do now?'

'You and Ramu shall share the *idli*,' said Alphonse.

The boy continued, 'I peeped and couldn't see him; I called and he wouldn't answer. I heard the tiger scratching something and growling. I came away . . .' He looked sad and anxious, moved aside and gobbled up the tiffin hurriedly.

The crowd, which watched in silence all along, let out a moan in chorus: 'Aiyo! Never thought our beloved headmaster would come to this end . . .' They all looked bitterly at the assistant headmaster, who they somehow held responsible for all the delay. The assistant headmaster probably had confused feelings, happy at the thought that after all he was getting his chance to become the headmaster, but also unhappy at the same time. He wailed the loudest at the thought of the headmaster's fate.

The commotion was at its height when Alphonse, properly armed with the permit, gave a final look to his double-barrelled gun, held it this way and that and looked through the barrel, and shouted a command; 'Your attention, everybody! Everyone must retreat at least a hundred yards before the school gate which will give you an initial advantage if the tiger should decide to chase. No one can foresee how the situation will develop. The beast when shot may smash the door and rush out, and God help anyone in its way. I'll count ten and this area must be cleared; otherwise, I won't be responsible for any calamity. Now all clear out . . . It's an emergency. The headmaster or whatever is left of him must be saved without delay. Now clear out, everyone.' He jingled the school-key bunch which he had snatched from the assistant headmaster. 'I'm risking my life . . . I'll push the door open and shoot the same second, normally that should be enough . . .' After this he let out a shout like a cattle-driver and a stampede started towards the gate, as he started counting: 'One, two, three . . .'

He turned to the chairman and his committee and said, as a special concession, 'You may stay back in that classroom to your left and watch through the window. I've reconnoitred that area; it'll be safe for you to stay there, and you will get a good view through the window, but make sure to bolt the door.' He said to Shekar, 'Boy, show them the room and stay there yourself with your friend, until I say "all clear". He may need two shots – the interval between the first one and the second will be crucial. Any-

[119]

thing may happen. No once can forecast with a hundred per cent certainty.'

After all these preliminaries, and before delivering the actual assault, Alphonse sat down on the veranda step and took a flask out of his hip pocket, muttering, 'This has been a big strain, must restore my nerves first . . .' He took a long swig out of it, while several pairs of eyes were watching him, smacked his lips, shook his head with satisfaction, picked up his gun and examined it keenly, and conducted a little rehearsal by pressing the butt against his shoulder and aiming at an imaginary tiger. He withdrew the gun and placed it at his side, took out the hip flask again, and took another long swig. He was heard to mutter, 'Hands are shaky, need steadying up.' And then he stood up with gun in hand, and rehearsed again with the butt against his shoulder. 'Still shaky . . . Bloody dilute rum, has no strength in it; I'll deal with that fellow.' He sat down again and took another drink, and another drink, till the flask was emptied.

My Master, who had stayed back unobtrusively, came forward to ask him, 'Whom were you talking to?'

'You,' said Alphonse. 'I knew you were here. I knew you'd not go. I saw you – you obstinate devil . . . So, I thought, I thought, what did I "thought"? I don't know. I have forgotten. No, no, if the beast comes out and swallows you, it'll serve you right . . . that's what I thought. Don't look at me like that . . . I'm not drunk . . . It's only watery rum . . . less than ten per cent proof . . . I'll deal with that cheat yet . . . that bastard . . .'

'Are you relaxing?' my Master asked.

'Yes, sir,' he said heartily.

And then my Master asked, 'What about the tiger?'

'What about what?'

'The tiger, the tiger in there . . .'

'Oh, yes, the tiger, he is O.K., I hope?'

'Aren't you going to shoot?'

'No,' he said emphatically. 'My hands must be steadied. I must have another drink. But my flask is empty. The son-of-a-bitch didn't fill it. I'll deal with him, don't worry. This sort of a thing . . .'

'The headmaster, what about him?'

'I don't know. Don't ask me. Am I responsible for every son-of-a-bitch?'

'Where did you learn this rare phrase?'

'In America,' he said promptly. 'I lived there for many years.'

'Would you like to rest?'

'Of course, how did you guess? I got up at four this morning and rode fifty miles. Where is my vehicle?'

My Master gave him a gentle push, and he fell flat on the ground and passed out.

My Master must have turned on him his powers of suggestion. Taking the key-bunch from Alphonse, he went up to the headmaster's room and had just inserted the key into the lock when the chairman, watching through the window, shouted across at the top of his voice, 'What are your trying to do? Stop!'

'I'm only trying to get the tiger out, so that the headmaster may come down confidently.'

While this was going on Shekar suddenly threw back the bolt of the classroom and rushed out, followed by his friend Ramu. Both of them came and stood over Alphonse, watching him wide-eyed. 'He is still breathing,' one said to the other.

Both of them asked my Master, 'Is Uncle dying?'

My Master said to them, 'No, he will wake up – but rather late – don't worry. He will be well again . . .'

'Why is he like this? A nice uncle . . .' the boy asked tearfully.

'Oh, he will be all right,' said my Master. 'Don't worry about him. He has drunk something that is not good and that has put him to sleep . . .'

'Is it toddy?' asked the boy.

'Maybe,' said my Master. 'What do you know about it?'

'There is a toddy shop near our house . . .' began the boy, and my Master listened patiently, while the boy described the scenes of drunkenness that he witnessed in the evenings. Finally the boys asked, 'How will he shoot the tiger?'

'No one is going to shoot,' said my Master. 'You will see the tiger come out and walk off with me . . .'

'He won't eat us?'

'No, he will not hurt anyone. I'm going to open the door and bring him out.'

'The headmaster?' the boy asked anxiously.

'He must have also fallen asleep. He will also come out . . . don't worry. Would you like to come in with me and see the tiger?'

The boy hesitated and, looking back for a safe spot, said, 'No, I'll stand there and watch.'

The chairman, who had watched this dialogue, cried from behind the window, 'What are you trying to do? You are mad.'

'Come out and be with me. You will see for yourself what I plan to do.'

'Explain,' the other cried. 'I do not understand you.'

My Master turned round, walked to the window, and asked, 'Are you afraid to come out of that room?'

'What a question!' exclaimed the chairman. 'Of course, who wouldn't be! We are in a hurry. The headmaster must have help without delay. We must act before the gunman wakes up . . .' He spoke through the window.

'Here, I have the key. I'll unlock the door and bring the tiger out of the room. One of you take a ladder in and help the headmaster come down from the attic. That's all . . .'

'Do you mean to say that you are going in as you are, without arms or protection?'

'Yes, that's what I'm going to do. We have no time to waste.'

The chairman said, 'By the powers vested in me in my capacity as the Second Honorary Magistrate in this town, I give you notice that you shall not open or enter that room. My committee members will bear witness to this order. It comes into immediate force, notwithstanding the fact that it's not yet in written form ...' He looked around at his members, who crowded near the window bars and assented in a chorus.

My Master asked when it subsided, 'Why'll you prevent me from going near the tiger?'

They were at a loss to answer: 'It's unlawful to commit suicide.'

'Maybe,' said my Master, 'but which law section says that a man should not approach a tiger? Are not circus people doing it all the time?'

'Yes,' replied the chairman weakly. 'But that's different.'

'I can tame a tiger as well as any circus ringmaster. It's after all my life that I'm risking.'

'There is no such thing as my life or your life before the eyes of the law: in the eyes of the law all lives are equal. No one can allow you to murder yourself ...'

'Life or death is in no one's hands: you can't die by willing or escape death by determination. A great power has determined the number of breaths for each individual, who can neither stop them nor prolong ... That's why God says in the *Gita*, "I'm life and death, I'm the killer and the killed ... Those enemies you see before you, O Arjuna, are already dead, whether you aim your arrows at them or not!"'

The chairman was visibly confused and bewildered. 'In that case you will have to sign an affidavit absolving us from all responsibilities for your life or death ...'

'You ignoramus of an honorary magistrate! After all that I have said, in spite of all that urgency ... All right, give me a paper and tell me what to write.'

The magistrate took out a sheet of paper from his briefcase and pushed it through the window bar. My Master sat down and wrote to the chairman's dictation through the window, absolving anyone from any responsibility. He signed the document and returned it with the comment, 'Just to respect your magistracy, although I am convinced it's uncalled-for and irrelevant, and you are exercising unnecessary authority. The more important thing for you now would be to take in your custody that gun beside Alphonse. When he wakes up, no one can guess his mood, and it's not safe to leave the gun within his reach.'

The chairman looked at the document and said, 'Stop, wait. Tell me what is it that you have written here?'

'Only what you have dictated.'

'In a language we don't know, can't accept it . . .'

'It's in Sanskrit, in which our scriptures are written, language of the gods. I write only Sanskrit although I know ten other languages including Japanese.' Without further ado, he turned round, paused for a second to satisfy himself that Alphonse was asleep, and put the key into the lock on the headmaster's room.

I had felt provoked at the sound of the key turning in the lock. No one had a right to come in and bother me. I was enjoying my freedom, and the happy feeling that the whip along with the hand that held it was banished for ever. No more of it; it was pleasant to brood over this good fortune. It was foolish of me to have let the whip go on so long. Next time anyone displayed the whip . . . I would know what to do. Just a pat with my paw, I realized, was sufficient to ward off any pugnacious design. What ignorance so far! Now that I knew what men were made of, I had confidence that I could save myself from them. The chair, ah, that was different. That was more paralysing than other instruments of torture. But here where I'm lying, the headmaster's room, there are chairs, much bigger and more forbidding than what Captain used to wield, but they have done nothing, they have not moved to menace or hurt me. They have stayed put. Now I've learnt much about chairs and men and the world in general. Perhaps these men were planning to trap me, cage me and force me to continue those jumping turns with the suspended lamb, shamelessly standing on my hind legs before the crowd of film-makers. If this was going to be the case, I must show them that I could be vicious and violent too. So far I had shown great concern and self-control. Thus far and no further. The evidence of my intentions should be the headmaster, who I hoped was somewhere above me, unharmed and, as I hoped, peacefully sleeping. I can't be definite. He makes no sort of sound or movement, hence I guess he must be sound asleep. I don't want to be disturbed, nor am I going to let anyone bother the headmaster. So I have a double responsibility now. Someone at the door. I held myself ready to spring forward.

The door opened quietly and my Master entered, shutting the door behind him. I dashed forward to kill the intruder, but I only hurt myself in hurling against the door. I fell back. He was not there, though a moment ago I saw him enter. I just heard him say, 'Understand that you are not a tiger, don't hurt yourself. I am your friend . . .' How I was beginning to understand his speech is a mystery. He was exercising some strange power over me. His presence sapped all my strength. When I made one more attempt to spring up, I could not raise myself. When he touched me, I tried to hit him, but my forepaw had no strength and collapsed like a rag. When I tried to snap my jaws, again I bit only the air. He merely said, 'Leave that style out. You won't have use for such violent gestures any more. It all goes into your past.' I had to become subdued, having no alternative, while he went on talking. 'It's a natural condition of existence. Every creature is born with a potential store of violence. A child, even before learning to walk, with a pat of its chubby hands just crushes the life out of a tiny ant crawling near it. And as he grows all through life he maintains a vast store of aggressiveness, which will be subdued if he is civilized, or expended in some manner that brings retaliation. But violence cannot be everlasting. Sooner or later it has to go, if not through wisdom, definitely through decrepitude, which comes on with years, whether one wants it or not. The demon, the tormentor, or the tyrant in history, if he ever survives to experience senility, becomes helpless and dependent, lacking the strength even to swat a fly. You are now an adult, full-grown tiger, and assuming you are fifteen years old, in human terms you would be over seventy years old, and at seventy and onwards one's temper gets toned down through normal decay, and let us be grateful for it. You cannot continue your ferocity for ever. You have to change . . .'

At this point someone from the other side of the door called, 'Sir, *Swamiji*, are you all right?'

'Yes, I am, don't you hear me talking?'

'Whom are you talking to, sir?'

'To a friendly soul,' he said.

'Do you mean the headmaster? Is he safe?'

'Yes, he is up there, but I've not begun to talk to him yet . . . he doesn't seem to be awake yet. I'll look to him presently. But at the moment I'm discoursing to the tiger . . .'

'Oh, oh, does it understand?'

'Why not? If you could follow what I've been saying, the tiger should understand me even better since I'm closer to his ear . . .' I let out a roar because I was feeling uncomfortable with some change coming inside me. I was beginning to understand. Don't ask me how. My Master never explained to me the mystery or the process of his influence on me.

'Don't let him out, sir,' said the voice. 'When you open the door, please warn us first . . .'

'Surely, if you are afraid, but let me tell you, you need not fear; he has only the appearance of a tiger, but he is not one – inside he is no different from you and me.' I felt restless and wanted to do something or at least get away from the whole situation, back to my familiar life, back to the jungle, to the bed of long grass – I sighed

[126]

for the feel of the grass on my belly – to the cool of the stream beside the cave and the shade of the cave with its rugged sandy floor . . . I was sick of human beings; they were everywhere, every inch of the earth seemed to be swarming with humanity; ever since the unfortunate day I stepped into that village in the forest to the present moment I was being hemmed in. How grand it'd be to be back in the world of bamboo shade and monkeys and jackals! Even the supercilious leopard and the owl I would not mind; compared to human company, they were pleasant, minding their own business, in spite of occasional moods to taunt and gossip.

I rose. Master became alert. 'What do you want to do now? You want to go away, I suppose! I understand. But there is no going back to your old life, even if I open the door and let you out. You can't go far. You will hurt others or you will surely be hurt. A change is coming, you will have to start a new life, a different one . . . Now lie down in peace, I will take you out. Let us go out together, it'll be safer. But first I must get the headmaster down from his perch. He has been there too long. Now you lie still, move away to the corner over there while I help him.'

I understood and slowly moved off to the side he indicated. Whatever its disadvantage, circus life had accustomed me to understand commands. This room was not too spacious to talk of far side and near side, but I obeyed him. I moved to the other wall and crouched there humbly. I wanted to show that I had no aggressive intentions. Now my Master ordered, 'Turn your face to the wall and do not stir in the least. If the headmaster thinks you are lifeless, so much the better. The situation is delicate, and you must do nothing to worsen it. God knows how long he has been cooped up there . . .'

He called him loudly but there was no answer. Then he went up to the door, opened it slightly and announced, 'I want a ladder and a person to climb to the loft, wake up the headmaster, and help him to come down. Is there anyone among you willing to fetch the ladder and go up?' A subdued discussion arose and a couple of men came forward to ask, 'What about the tiger? Where is he?'

'You have all improved to the extent of not referring to him as "brute" or "beast", but I'm sorry to note that you still have no confidence in him or me. Let me assure you that this tiger will harm no one.' This had no effect on anyone. There was no response. He said, 'All right, I'll manage . . .' He shut the door again, pulled the table into position, and put up a chair on it, then another chair and a stool, and went up step by step and reached the loft, saying to himself, 'How the headmaster reached here will remain a mystery . . .' He grasped the edge of the loft and heaved himself up.

Presently I heard him waking the headmaster and coaxing him to climb down. I could not see his actual coming down as I had to lie facing the wall; I could only hear movements and words. My Master exerted all his power to persuade him to step down. I sensed what was happening and though curious to watch, did not turn round, as I did not want to disobey my Master. The first thing the headmaster did on coming down was to cry, 'Oh, it's still here!' and I heard some scurrying of feet, and my Master saying, 'Don't look at him, but step down; he will not attack.' The headmaster groaned and whimpered and was possibly trying to go back to the loft, at which my Master must have toppled the pile of chairs and pulled him down. I heard a thud and guessed that the poor man had landed on firm ground. I could hear him moaning, 'It is still there, how can I?' My Master kept advising, 'What if it is still there? Don't look in its direction, turn away your head, come with me . . .' He led the headmaster as he kept protesting, a sorry spectacle, in disarray, still in the coat and turban which he had worn in the morning. My Master propelled him to the door and pushed him out saying to those outside, 'Here he is, take care of him. Not a scratch, only shock . . .' and shut the door again as a medley of comments, questions, and exclamations poured into the room.

Now he addressed me. 'Now turn round, get up, and do whatever you like.' I stretched myself, yawned, and rose to my feet. That was all I could do. I felt grateful, but I could not make out his form clearly. There was a haze in which he seemed to exist, a haze that persisted all through our association. At no time could I be certain of his outline or features – except what I could gather from his talk. He said, 'Let us go out now. You must realize that human beings for all their bluster are timid creatures, and are likely to get into a panic when they see you. But don't look at them. This is one of the rules of yoga to steady one's mind, to look down one's nose and at nothing beyond. That's one way not to be distracted and to maintain one's peace of mind. I would ask you to keep your head bowed and cast your eyes down and make no sort of sound, whatever may be the reaction of the people we pass. We are bound to meet crowds during our passage through the town. People are likely to get excited at the sight of us, but you must notice nothing.'

This was a necessary instruction since our emergence from the room created a sensation and a stampede, in spite of the warning cry my Master had given: 'Now I am coming out with the tiger. Those who are afraid, keep away, but I assure you again that Raja will not attack anyone. He will walk past you, and you will be quite safe as if a cat passed by. Believe me. Otherwise keep out of the way. I'll give you a little time to decide.' When he opened the door, he said, 'Keep close to me.' As he stepped out of the room, I was at his heels, saw no one, but only heard suppressed, excited comments and whispers from different corners. The veranda was empty, not a soul in sight, with the exception of Alphonse lying on the top step. Without a word my Master walked on briskly. We had to brush past Alphonse. The breeze of our movement seemed to have blown on his face, and he immediately sat up, rubbed his eyes to see clearly, blinked, shook his head and muttered, 'Crazy dream!' and laid himself down and apparently went back to sleep. But he sat up again to watch us go. We had gone past him a little way when he cried, 'Hey, you bearded one, you again! Won't leave me alone even in a dream! Ah! What is this?'

'Tiger,' answered my Master.

'Is it the same or another one?' asked Alphonse.

'Same and another,' answered my Master cryptically.

'How? Oh, yes, of course,' he muttered, puzzled.

'You may touch the tiger if you like.'

'No, no! Go away.' He waved us off angrily and resumed his sleep.

At first, when the Master emerged from the school gate with the tiger, the crowds in the street stood petrified. Cycles, automobiles, lorries and bullock-carts hurriedly withdrew to the side; even street dogs slunk away under culverts after whining feebly. As advised by the Master, the tiger never lifted its eyes but followed his steps. The Master passed down quickly, reached the Market Gate, turned to his right, proceeded northward on the highway, and vanished at dusk towards the mountains.

Gradually lorries and bullock-carts began to move, cyclists resumed their wobbly courses, and crowds reappeared on Market Road; at street corners people stood about in clusters regaling each other with sensational accounts of the day's events, while mischievous urchins continued to run up and down Market Road screaming, 'Tiger! Tiger! It's here again!'

At Anand Bhavan, which had already had a visitation, the main door was closed, but guests were admitted through a back door, the proprietor whispering as they entered, 'Finish your business soon and be off . . . remember, no talk of tiger any more . . . have had enough . . .'

At the Boardless, however, it was different. The din in the hall was deafening, but Mr Varma, the proprietor, who, from the eminence of his cash desk, always enjoyed listening to his clients' voices, felt especially gratified today with the medley of comments, questions, and arguments falling on his ears while his fingers cease-lessly counted cash.

'That hermit must have come from the Himalayas. I have heard that there are many extraordinary souls residing in the ice caves, capable of travelling any distance at will, and able to control any-thing by their yogic powers.'

'How could the yogi have known that there was a tiger in the headmaster's room, and why should he have wanted to protect it?'

'Probably they were family friends!' They laughed at the joke.

'It may be no laughing matter. I was at the school and could overhear his conversation with the tiger as if it were his younger brother.'

'Don't be too sure. Suppose that tiger makes a meal of his brother and turns round for more. We must be watchful – where are the police? Why can't they come out of their hiding and patrol the streets?'

'I tried to see the headmaster in Vinayak Street; after all he had kept longer company with the tiger than anyone else. But he was incoherent and still nervous lest the tiger should spring out of the next room. He had to be carried home in Gaffur's taxi, you know.'

'The question remains, who is this tiger-tamer – the terrible animal trots behind him, while the circus-wallah for all his expert control could not save himself in the end.'

'Whenever we questioned "Who are you?" he quipped and dodged, you know,' said a pedagogue.

Jayaraj, who framed pictures sitting in a cubicle at the Market Arch, observed the goings-on in the town from his position of vantage, and had spent a lifetime commenting and gossiping while his hands were busy nailing picture frames. He was now explaining to a company at the centre table, 'At first I didn't close my shop. I was not going to be frightened into thinking that the tiger would come to eat me or the glass sheets in my shop. But when I saw the crowd flooding past, I too caught the frenzy, and went there rather late but just in time to see that man come out of the school with his pet. The crowd pressed me against the gate post, I could not back away farther when the tiger almost brushed past my legs and I shivered, wedged as I was between the animal and the wall. When he noticed my fright that man just said, "Don't fear", and passed on, but in that instant I recognized him – the shape of those eyes, the voice, and those features were familiar, and through all that shrunken frame and sunburnt, hairy face, I could see who he was. After all I had started life as a photographer, and when one has looked at faces through a lens, one can never forget a face.

'At one time I used to see him cycling up the Market Road every morning to his college. He lived in Ellamman Street in one of those solid houses built by an earlier generation. I can't remember that man's name now, Govind, Gopal, or Gund? I don't know. He was arrested during the Independence Movement for climbing the Collector's office roof and tearing down the Union Jack, and then again for inscribing on the walls, with brush and tar, "Quit India", aimed at the British. I was told that he drove his mother mad by his ways. She would cry her heart out every time he was sent to prison. He didn't pass his B.A. – too busy, mixed up as he was in every kind of demonstration in those days. When things quietened down after Independence, he came to me one day to have his passport photo taken, but never collected it, though he had paid for it in advance. His photo must still be there somewhere in those piles of stuff unclaimed by my customers for reasons best known to them. I must put them all to the fire some day before all that junk drives me out of my own shop . . .

'Later on, I used to see him occasionally coming to the market with his family, driving a motor car. At this stage, he was completely changed, looked like a fop with his tie and suit and polished shoes. One day I had the hardihood to hail him and to say that he should take away his passport photograph, since he had paid for it. I'm not the sort to keep other people's property. He halted his steps but before I could pick up his stuff and pack it, he muttered "I will come again" and hurried out. He was perhaps a busy man, as he was said to be holding a big job in a foreign insurance firm which had its office in New Extension.

'I never thought of him again until I heard one day that he had vanished, abandoning his wife and children. The police came seeking his photograph but I didn't give it. If that man chose to disappear, that was his business, why should I be involved?'

'Any reason why he went away?'

'I know as much as you do. Why ask me? Enough . . . talk of something else . . . Let us forget him and his tiger. Something uncanny about him . . . unsafe to talk about such men, who may be saints or sorcerers. Who knows what will happen? Remember the ancient saying, "Don't probe too far into the origin of a river or a saint! You will never reach the end." ' With that Jayaraj abruptly got up, paid for his coffee, and went away.

'Extraordinary how that animal could not be shot at all,' mused someone after Jayaraj left. 'Alphonse, who had hunted tigers all his life, fell into a stupor when he lifted his gun today.'

'Oh! Oh! Stupor indeed,' someone said, laughing.

Late in the evening Alphonse woke up on the school steps, looked around, and muttered, 'Not a soul in sight. Where is everybody gone? They have bluffed me.' He got up, went over to his motor cycle, and kicked the starter viciously. Entering the Market Junction, he noticed people standing in knots and slowed down to shout, 'Why don't you keep out of the way?'

'The tiger is gone,' someone ventured to inform him over the roar of his motor cycle. He replied, 'Oh, shut up, all that nonsense about the tiger! It is over a year since I saw one. Those bastards have April-Fooled us. They would not even let me peep through the keyhole to see for myself. I will deal with them yet.'

'But it seems you did see the tiger from the rooftop?' ventured his listener.

'You don't have to tell me what I see or don't see, understand? None of your business. If ever you see a real tiger with a tail at the right end, call me; otherwise it is a waste of time.' With that Alphonse was off.

We passed through many villages, big and small, towards I don't know where, as I followed my Master; everywhere people made way for us, retreated hurriedly, staring in wonder and disbelief, afraid even to breathe. Crowds which would normally be noisy and jostle looked intimidated by the spectacle, which made my Master remark, 'What our country needs most is a tiger for every village and town to keep people disciplined . . .' In some places someone would call out from afar, 'Tiger-man, put a collar and chain around your pet – we are terrified . . .'

'Come and do it yourself,' my Master said. 'I will have no objection and I can tell this tiger to remain still while you collar it . . .'

We passed on while I stuck close to his heels and moved along without lifting my head or looking at anyone too long. My Master told me, 'The eye is the starting point of all evil and mischief. The eye can travel far and pick out objects indiscriminately, mind follows the eye, and rest of the body is conditioned by the mind. Thus starts a chain of activity which may lead to trouble and complication, or waste of time, if nothing else; and so don't look at anything except the path.' Sometimes I could not resist looking at cattle or other creatures, which I would normally view as my rightful prize. But I'd immediately avert my eyes when I realized what I was doing.

We were about to descend the slope of a hillock when we noticed in the valley below a procession passing. People were dragging a flower-decorated chariot with pipes and drums. The chariot carried the image of God, and there was much rejoicing and dancing and singing, and scattering of flowers. Vendors of fruits or sweets were doing a brisk business with the children swarming around. But the moment we were seen, everyone ran for safety. God's chariot was abandoned in the middle of the road; the drummers and pipers abruptly stopped their music and, clutching their instruments, ran madly. My Master said to me, 'Stay here, and don't move even if people come near or touch you.' He left me there and ran forward and said to those on the run, 'Come, come back, don't abandon your God. Draw the chariot along. Come on, come on. My tiger is godly, and loves a procession.' He went after the piper and the drummer, and brought them back forcibly, saying, 'That tiger of ours is musically inclined, and won't like to be cheated out of it Go on, play your pipes. This tiger is no real tiger at all. He just looks like one, that's all. He loves you all. Go on . . .' With their gaze fixed in my direction they played nervously. The chariot wheels moved again and the crowd followed, although in a subdued spirit. The children did not laugh or dance; the sweet-sellers did not cry their wares. 'This pains me very much, how can I prove you are a friend?' said my Master, falling back. We took a detour and went forward.

At another place we went into a rioting mob – groups of people were engaged in a bloody strife, attacking each other with stone, knife, and iron rod, and screaming murderous challenges. In their frenzy they had not noticed us, but when they did, they dispersed swiftly. My Master cried to them, 'If I find you fighting again, I'll be back to stop it. Take care. You should not need a tiger to keep the peace.'

When we reached the foot of Mempi range, he looked up with joy at a towering peak in front of us and said, 'That ought to be our home, but it is inaccessible, so we will stop here . . . I was here before, and once saw a flash of light on the very tip of that peak and felt overwhelmed by its mystery since no human being has ever set foot there. Although I realize now that it might be no more than a touch of the moon rising behind it, I will still

[135]

watch for it: I have a great desire to see that flash again . . .'

He searched and found his spot. A rock jutting over a ledge seemed to him adequate shelter. He said, 'Here we will stay.' He broke some twigs and swept the floor. Farther off there was a spring bubbling up from a cavity in the rock. 'You can have a drink of water here, but I cannot tell you where you should seek your food. I don't know and I do not wish to think of it, as I cannot give you any help. I know I cannot persuade you to eat grass or live on roots and greens. God has decided for you a difficult diet. I can help your mind and soul, but I cannot affect your body or its functions. Now I should leave you free to go where you like, but don't go too far away from here or too long . . .'

I accepted his advice. All day long I lay across the entrance of his shelter. It was enough for me that I was near him, while he sat with his eyes shut in prayer. I cannot say how long he would sit thus. In the evenings he would open his eyes, and then talk to me on life and existence and death, and help my understanding. More than once he mentioned God. The word 'God' had been unheard of by me. We who live in the jungle have never known the word. He explained God; most of it was beyond my understanding, but he said, 'You may not understand the word. But let it sink in your mind and ring on your ears, and then tell me later how you feel.' He described God in his own terms as the Creator, the Great Spirit pervading every creature, every rock and tree and the sky and the stars; a source of power and strength. Later when my Master questioned me about it, I said that God must be an enormous tiger, spanning the earth and the sky, with a tail capable of encircling the globe, claws that could hook on the clouds, and teeth that could grind the mountain, and possessing, of course, immeasurable strength to match. On hearing my notion of God, my Master burst into a laugh and said, 'It's often said that God made man in His own image, it's also true that man makes God in his own image. Both may be right; and you are perfectly right in thinking of your

God as a super tiger. Also it may be true. What we must not forget is that He may be everything we imagine and more. In *Bhagavad Gita* He reveals Himself in a mighty terrifying form which pervades the whole universe in every form of life and action. Remember also He is within every one of us and we derive our strength from Him . . .' He did not treat me as an animal which sat before him in respectful silence trying to understand his words; I only felt grateful that he was trying to transform me in so many ways. How he could do it was his own secret.

At dawn, it was his habit to go to the spring and bathe, wash his single piece of cloth, and wear it, allowing it to dry on his body. He would then pray and meditate, and break off to go into the forest and return with an armful of roots, herbs, and leaves which provided him nourishment. Except those moments when he discoursed to me, he remained silent and often went into deep meditation. Nowadays the keenness of my hunger was also gone, and I slipped away into the jungle, not too often, only when I felt I could not stand hunger any more. When I returned from my hunt, I kept myself away until he summoned me. I would be oppressed with a sense of guilt in spite of the fact that when I hunted and killed, I was lost in the thrill of the moment and relished the taste of warm flesh and blood, a luxury I had missed at the circus, where stale meat was thrown out of buckets at feeding time, by butchers on contract. It might be any meat, no way of knowing, might be a dog's or a donkey's, dull-tasting since the contractor soaked the meat in water to give it weight. So all along I could not help craving for fresh kill. But nowadays, the moment I had eaten my fill I'd be seized with remorse. And so, when I returned from the jungle I'd lie low, out of sight of my Master.

Even for drinking water, I chose another stream within the forest, since I did not want to sully the spring in which my Master performed his morning ablutions. Nor would my Master shame me by referring to my night expeditions. I tried to attain some kind of purification by reducing the frequency of seeking food. Nor did I kill recklessly as I used to in my jungle days – any game of any size or bulk, I used to slaughter, consume it partly, and return to the fly-covered remnant again the next day. I could not bear to recollect this habit: it nauseated. Nowadays, I went into the jungle and stalked the littlest game, just sufficient enough to satisfy my hunger of the moment and not my gluttony. And then I didn't go into the forest again for several days, prolonging the intervals as much as possible. I suffered hunger for consecutive days before seeking food again, but felt nobler for it. I felt I had attained merit through penance, making myself worthy of my Master's grace. How I wished I had learnt the art of living on sugar cane and rice, like the elephant and the hippo of the circus; the chimp would explain how they ate nothing else, which lesson I should have taken from them. How mighty the hippo and the elephant looked, although they ate no meat.

At night I quietly returned to a spot beyond a screen of vegetation not far from my Master, ready to reach his side in a few bounds if summoned. This phase of life I found elevating: the change churning internally was still felt by me, but did not bother me now as it did at the beginning. I was getting accustomed to many changes. If I could have shed the frightening physical encasement God has chosen for me, I could have lived on air, or dry leaves, and I'd have felt more blessed. Understanding the turmoil in me, my Master said, 'Do not crave for the unattainable. It's enough you have realization. All in good time. We cannot understand God's intentions. All growth takes place in its own time. If you brood on your improvements rather than your shortcomings, you will be happier.'

While I learnt a great deal from my Master, enough to know myself, understand the world in which I lived, feel and express my thoughts (although understood only by my Master), one thing he would not teach me was the art of reckoning. Numbers and figures were still beyond my grasp. To my questioning, he said, 'Why do you want to know how long ago or before or how much later or earlier? Not necessary for you. A sense of time may be required for human beings engaged in worldly activities. But why for you and me? I shun all activities and you have none. You have freed yourself from all duties which had been forced on you. And so you need not know what time of the day or what time of the week, or numbers, reckoning of before and after, when and how far; in short you don't have to know the business of counting, which habit has made us human beings miserable in many ways. We have lost the faculty of appreciating the present living moment. We are always looking forward or backward and waiting for one or sighing for the other, and lose the pleasure of awareness of the moment in which we actually exist. Time is not for you or for that matter me, although at some stage of my life . . .' Here was some hint of his past life and I pricked up my ears. He understood that I wished to know more about him. 'Why do you want to know what I was or how or where? It'd be unnecessary knowledge. Knowledge, like food, must be taken within limits. You must know only as much as you need, and not more. All the thousands of human beings you have encountered since leaving the shelter of your forest life suffer from minds overburdened with knowledge, facts, and information – fetters and shackles for the rising soul.

'I was a man of the world, busy and active and living by the clock, scrutinizing my bank book, greeting and smiling at all and sundry because I was anxious to be treated as a respectable man in society. One day it seemed all wrong, a senseless repetition of activities, where one's head always throbbed with the next plan, counting time or money or prospects – and I abruptly shed everything including (but for a bare minimum) clothes, and fled away from wife, children, home, possessions, all of which seemed intolerable. At midnight, I softly drew the bolt of our back door, opening on the sands of Sarayu behind our house at Ellamman

[139]

Street, while others slept and left very much in the manner of Siddhartha ... They searched but gave up eventually, concluding that I was washed off in the Sarayu, which was in flood at that time ... I trudged and tramped and wandered through jungles and mountains and valleys not caring where I went. I achieved complete anonymity, and shed purpose of every kind, never having to ask what next. And so here I am, that's all you need to know.'

Although my Master had taken the trouble to choose a remote part of the jungle to live in, people seemed to have got scent of us, of the novelty of our life – a man living in the company of a tiger – and began to visit us. The news must have spread from village to village. One morning, watching from his ashram, a sort of table at an elevation, which could give one a view of the surrounding country, we saw a file of peasants approaching at a distance. My Master remarked, 'No escape from humanity! They'll pursue you even if you hide yourself in the bowels of the earth. Anyway, you keep yourself out of view so that they may approach without fear.' I had been lying on the ground while he sat on the slab of stone. I got up in obedience to his command and moved off to my cave behind the screen of creepers and *lantana* shrubs. Presently I noticed from my spot some men arrive, carrying baskets of flowers and fruits. They stood away at a distance and hallooed: '*Swamiji*, are you there?'

'Yes, I'm here, but I am no *Swamiji*.'

'May we approach you?'

'Why not? Anyone is welcome.'

'But you have the tiger with you still?'

'Yes, naturally, but he is not a tiger.'

'He looks like one, we are afraid.'

'Then why do you want to come?'

'For your *darshan*, sir.' This kind of talk went on for a while. 'Don't use the word *darshan*,' he shouted back.

'Why not, master?'

'Because the word is not appropriate . . .'

'What does *darshan* actually mean, sir? We do not wish to offend you.'

'Why don't you come up and ask, so that I may not have to shout through my answer.'

'Of course, sir, we are naturally here to sit at your feet . . .'

Master uttered an exclamation of impatience. 'Oh, at my feet! Where have you picked up these phrases of mental slavery? Come up if you are not afraid. What makes you think you are safe there if it's the tiger that frightens you? He can easily come there too – nothing to hold him back.'

'Have you not tied him up, sir?'

'Certainly not, I live freely too . . . so there is no place in my system for any rope or chain or bond of any kind. If you don't muster enough courage and confidence, turn back and go.'

'We have come a long way, sir, for your *dar* –' They were about to say '*darshan*' again but restrained themselves.

'I leave you to your discretion. Go back if you like . . .'

But they hesitated uncertainly, and consulted among themselves. Having taken the trouble to come so far, they didn't want to waste the visit, and perhaps feeling that they might encounter the tiger in any case even while retreating, in a short while they came up and placed their offerings before my Master. When he noticed their preparations to prostrate before him, he said emphatically. 'I won't allow you to prostrate.' They would not listen to his objection. In spite of it, they threw themselves full-length on the ground and tried to touch his feet. He shrank back from them and threw himself on the ground as a counter-measure and tried to take the dust off their feet. They scrambled up in great confusion. 'Oh, *Swamiji*, you could not do it. We are small men, but you are great.'

'How? Because I'm unshaven and shirtless? I don't shave because I find it easier not to. I don't wear a shirt because I don't have one.

But for these, I go about with the tiger because it's God's will. I am not different from you, we are equals and no need to pay homage to me. It has no meaning. You must prostrate only before God. You should seek only God's *darshan*, we must not misappropriate the word that belongs to him, in a temple. Even that I doubt, since the same God resides within all of us. When you address a prayer to God, you are only praying to yourself ... or at least you are entitled to half that prayer; and if you are offering a flower, again half is yours, as a famous mystic poet sung ...' At this point he suddenly lifted his head and delivered a full-throated song, his voice rebounding from the rocks. 'When I bring my palms together and raise my arm in prayer, I'm only half-praying to you. Is it right to pray thus?'

His visitors were overwhelmed, but suddenly remembered the tiger and asked timidly, 'Where is the tiger?'

'Don't think of him. Sit down with an easy mind and tell me your purpose. Why do you spoil your mind with thoughts of the tiger? Having come all this distance ...'

They placed the basket of flowers and fruits before him and appealed, 'Please accept these.'

He took just a single flower and a small banana. 'Yes, these will do. Take them back to the children in your village, and the flowers to the womenfolk.'

They sat down again on the ground in front of my Master and began to explain. 'We are from both the sides you found fighting the other day. We have come to assure you that we will not fight again. When your honour passed through our village that day, you saw us in a shameful state ... We are here to beg your forgiveness.'

'Ask God's forgiveness rather than mine.'

'The cause of our fight that day –'

'Don't tell me what – all causes of rivalry and clash are senseless and so need no defining or explanation ... Don't ever fight. No cause is worth a clash.'

'We pledge never to fight again. Your gracious presence helped us the other day . . .'

'That's good. You should not depend upon a tiger or a bearded man again to help you settle your differences. If you are ready to hate and want to destroy each other, you may find a hundred reasons – a diversion of canal water in your field, two urchins of opposite camps slapping each other, rumours of molestation of some woman, even the right to worship in a temple, anything may spark off a fight if you are inclined to nurture hatred – only the foolish waste their lives in fighting . . .'

One morning I was lying at the feet of my Master; he was sitting in meditation. Nowadays he encouraged me to remain close by when he meditated as it might help me too. At such moments a profound silence prevailed, and the sublime state to which he had raised his mind carried mine also along. At such moments I felt lighter at heart and my physical self also became secondary. My sight became clearer; if I lifted my gaze to the horizon, the sun shining on the land filled me with joy: the leaves of the mighty banyan trees sparkling like gems, the bamboos swaying their golden stems with their filigreed leaves – I felt I could ask for nothing more in life. When he read the state of my mind, my Master explained. 'No one would credit a tiger with so much poetic joy, it is inconceivable. Looking back, I would say that in one of your previous births you might have been a poet, and your deeper personality retains that *vasana* still. Whatever one had thought or felt is never lost, but is buried in one's personality and carried from birth to birth. You must have been a poet, perhaps many centuries ago in the court of a king, your shoulder wrapped in a resplendent shawl, a diamond bracelet on your arm, seated beside the throne stirring royal hearts with songs of nightingale, moon, roses or of an aching heart pining away for the lost love . . . Oh, Raja, I see a visitor coming up, of all things a woman, go, hide yourself before

[143]

she sees you, she may faint in my arms . . .' I rose and went behind the screen of *lantana* bush and the rock.

Presently the visitor arrived, panting. I could see her through the foliage. I couldn't describe a human being. My Master never taught me how to distinguish one from another. All humans look alike in my eyes, and my Master has confirmed that it is the right view. I could, in a rough manner, identify some special personalities like Captain or the clowns or Rita by prolonged association, and especially by their functions. If I needed to know the looks of any person, I would know it only through my Master's description. When he understood my curiosity about this woman, he explained that she was over fifty years old, medium height, dark, round cheeks, with grey hair tied up at the back.

The lady advanced towards my Master, seated on his slab of stone, and prostrated.

'Madam, you should not prostrate before me, please get up. I never like anyone to touch my feet.'

She got up, saying, 'One has the right to show one's veneration for a sublime soul, a saint perhaps.'

'Please sit down, madam. I am unhappy that I can offer you only the bare ground to sit on, no carpet or mat.'

'They're immaterial, the great thing is to be blessed with your *darshan*.'

'Calm yourself, rest for a while, you don't have to say anything. Feel completely free to remain silent. You don't have to utter a single word.'

The lady smiled. 'I've not come all the way to observe a vow of silence.'

'Perhaps I may be under a vow not to hear a word . . .'

'Quite likely . . . even then I will speak since I have come all the way.'

'By all means. Go ahead. I have not shut off my ears yet. First let me ask what brought you here?'

[144]

'I heard of a remarkable person who went out with a tiger, as if he had taken a dog out, and I told myself I must see this *Swamiji*, it's only this remarkable man who can help me in my search . . .'

'Don't you see what risk you face by going after a *sadhu* you have only heard about? He might be a fake.'

'Yes, I fear that too,' she said.

'You might be endangering your virtue, too . . .'

'At my age and condition, my virtue is quite safe. No one will be tempted to molest a grey-haired fat hag. Only they robbed me of the money I had, and also a chain and bangles; while crossing a lonely forest path, three men accosted me, and relieved me of my jewellery and a bundle of clothes, too, and went their way quietly. Good men, they only robbed, which seems to me less heinous than deserting one's family and home for no reason.'

'How can you say "no reason"? An inner compulsion is enough to make one take fateful decisions.'

How I wished I could join their conversation. Not only could I not speak, but I had to keep my cursed form concealed behind the *lantana* bush in order not to scare the visitor. If permitted, I would have asked, 'How did you come to know about my Master?'

As if in answer to my question, she was saying, 'On that day when a tiger was at school, I went there with a neighbour who was searching for her son. The crowd was pressing and suffocating, pushing us about. Everybody was terrified, and yet wanted to get a glimpse of the tiger, with the result no one could ever go in. My companion broke down and wept helplessly. Some mischievous persons were enjoying the situation by suddenly crying out, "Run, run, the tiger has come, the tiger is coming," and kept the crowd running back and forth. I and my friend got separated in the mêlée. Later when we met, she told me how she was comforted and helped by a bare-bodied *sadhu* who was calmly sitting on a culvert outside the school gate.'

'In what manner did the *sadhu* help her?'

'He told her that the tiger was locked in and would not harm anyone, and also that her son must be with the other children safely sheltered in the school hall. Was that *sadhu* you?'

'Could be, or might be any other bare-bodied, bearded person. There must be hundreds of them everywhere.'

'But there was only one in that place and he was offering to lead away the tiger.'

'Oh, did he?'

'And something that she had noticed about him which she mentioned made me think.'

'What could it be?'

'He was in the habit of rubbing his finger across his brow while thinking, as you are doing now . . .'

It was true, when my Master was listening or thinking he always drew his finger across his brow as if writing something there. The mention of this mannerism seemed to disturb my Master's equanimity, but only for a moment; he laughed and said, 'This is my habit, surely I know it. I do it and a hundred others may also be doing it, just to probe what's written there by fate, like a blind man's running his finger over an etching, and are we not all blind where our fates are concerned?'

'By the time I learnt about the *sadhu*, he was gone with his tiger. I went back home and kept thinking. The picture came up before me as to how I had not seen anyone else do it. How when he sat in the veranda, reclining in his easy chair, reading a newspaper, he'd hold it in one hand so as to leave the other free to trace his forehead; or before going out to his office, if I asked for cash for some domestic shopping, he would always say, "If I could conjure up the money," and while uttering the word "conjure", he'd send his fingers dancing across his forehead – whether joking or serious, he always took his fingers to his forehead. I have also felt sometimes irritated by it and told him, "Oh, keep off your fingers from your head, it's very distracting!" When our son had a problem in his college, you could

not listen to him without these fingers almost skinning your forehead.'

'Did he help his son at all?'

'The boy was in constant trouble with a particular master who
was rather vindictive, but you went up to their principal and spoke
to him and from that day –'

'You are beginning, I now notice, to use the word "you", which
is not proper; keep to "he".'

'Even now I notice your fingers going to your brow . . .'

'Many people have that habit, you see of all organs, it is the
hand that's most active and independent. The hand acts by itself
when you are not watchful – it can tease you by hiding the keys . . .
It's the hand that goes forward first to strangle a throat, fondle a
lover, or bless or thieve . . . If God had devised the hand differently,
the world and human actions and attitudes would have been
different.'

She was listening with adoration. At this moment I sneezed,
some insect having settled on my nostril. She asked in alarm, 'What
is that?'

'Oh, some jungle noise, don't worry about it.'

'Oh, husband, how can you forget the years we have spent
together, twenty years, twenty-five, thirty – I have lost count . . .'

'Don't say "husband", it is a wrong word . . .'

'Husband, husband, husband, I'll repeat it a thousand times and
won't be stopped. I know to whom I'm talking. Don't deceive me
or cheat me. Others may take you for a hermit, but I know you
intimately. I have borne your vagaries patiently for a lifetime: your
inordinate demands of food and my perpetual anxiety to see you
satisfied, and my total surrender night or day when passion seized
you and you displayed the indifference of a savage, never caring for
my health or inclination, and with your crude jocularities even
before the children, I shudder!'

'You should have felt happy to lose such a husband. Why have

[147]

you gone after him? No reason, especially when he has left for you and your children a comfortable home, all the money he had, and every kind of security in life. If you think over it, you will realize that the surrender has been rather on his part: it was total, he took nothing for himself except a piece of loin-cloth for all the wealth he had accumulated! However, please know that he left home not out of wrath, there was no cause for it, but out of an inner transformation.'

'You have a strange way of talking now.'

He said with a touch of firmness, 'Time for you to start back if you must reach the nearest village before nightfall. I'll take you down and from the village you can go on.'

'I can't go without you—or let me stay with you . . .'

'Impossible. What you see is my old shell; inside it's all changed. You can't share my life.'

'Come home with me, I'll accept you as you are, keep your beard and loin-cloth, only let me have my husband at home . . .'

'Listen attentively: my past does not exist for me, nor a future. I live for the moment, and that awareness is enough for me. To attain this state, I have gone through much hardship. I don't have to explain all that now. I have erased from my mind my name and identity and all that it implies. It would be unthinkable to slide back. You must live your own life and leave me to live mine and end it my own way.'

She broke down and wailed aloud. He calmly watched her. 'I wish I could help you, as I managed to help Raja and calm his turbulent soul. I can only pray for your well-being.'

'Let me stay in that village, so that I'll at least be near you.'

'Why should you? You can't. You have your own home and family.'

'Have you no feeling or even an ordinary sense of duty?'

'I do not understand these phrases. I have forgotten the meaning of many words. Please do not force me to talk so much about

[148]

myself. Because of my sympathies and a real desire to help you, I have spoken. Otherwise I never revive the identity of the past in thought or word; it's dead and buried.'

'You are callous; you talk of sympathy just with the tip of your tongue. You have no real feeling, you are selfish, you are . . .' She went on until sheer exhaustion overcame her.

He listened to her in stony silence. At some point he even failed to look at her; closed his eyes and went into meditation. He just said, 'I'll take you down to the village. Let's get there before sunset.'

'Why should you take the trouble?'

'You will have to pass through the jungle all alone.'

'I can go alone, as I came . . .'

'Yes, we come into the world alone, and are alone while leaving. Your understanding is becoming deeper.'

She repeated, 'I didn't need your help while coming. Why should you bother about a stranger? You and your tiger – if he is there in the jungle and meets me, I shall be grateful if he ends my misery then and there, or couldn't you tell him?'

'You will reach home safely.'

She sprang to her feet. 'Finally, is there no way I can persuade you?'

'I need no persuasion . . . God be with you.'

She wiped her eyes with the end of her sari, turned round, hurried down the hill, and disappeared into the jungle. He sat motionless in his seat and closed his eyes in meditation.

I did not wish to disturb him; I kept away until he should call me. I didn't go out to hunt that night, preferring to go without food. I didn't want to go prowling in the forest for fear that if that lady happened to be there and saw me, she might die of shock.

My Master never mentioned her visit again. He sat continuously in meditation for a few days, and then our normal life was resumed. He bathed in the pool, went into the forest to gather roots and leaves for his nourishment, meditated and discoursed to me in the evenings seated on his slab of stone.

Thus life went on. As I have said I have no reckoning of time. I could only measure it by my own condition. Gradually I realized that I was becoming less inclined to get up and move, preferring to spend long hours in my own corner hidden behind the shrub. I preferred to go without food rather than undergo the strain of chasing game. I could not run fast enough to catch anything. Many creatures eluded me with ease. Most of my old associates, the langur, the jackal, and others who used to watch me and annoy, were missing, perhaps dead or not frequenting this particular part of the forest. My claws sometimes stuck and most of my teeth had fallen. It was difficult for me to tear or chew. My movements were becoming so slow and clumsy that I was often outwitted; and when I succeeded in cornering some animal, I could not kill it successfully. I took a long time to consume it. The result was that in due course, I was underfeeding myself and my skin fell in folds.

My hearing was also impaired. Nowadays I could not hear when my Master summoned me. And his discourses were much reduced as he understood that I could not hear him properly. He told me, 'Raja, old age has come on you. Beautiful old age, when faculties are dimmed one by one, so that we may be restful, very much like extinguishing lights in a home, one by one, before one goes to sleep. Listen attentively. You may live a maximum of five years; I don't think we should risk your suffering starvation or attack from other creatures or hunters. Once they know you are old and weak, they will come for you and you are going to be alone because we are about to part. Last night I realized that the time for my attaining *samadhi* is near at hand. I must prepare for it by releasing myself from all bondage . . . As a first step, I'm releasing you. Tomorrow a man will come to take charge of you. He is the head of a zoo in the town. You will spend the rest of your years in the company of animals. You will be safe in a cage, food will be brought to you, and they will open the door and let you out to move freely in an open-air enclosure, and look after you.' Never having been in the habit of questioning my Master, I accepted his plans, though with a heavy heart. He explained his philosophy: 'No relationship, human or other, or association of any kind could last for ever. Separation is the law of life right from the mother's womb. One has to accept it if one has to live in God's plans.'

Very soon we had a visitor from the town. It was noon. The visitor looked to me a kindly person; he held no whip in hand. He had a companion and down below on the forest track there was a cage on wheels. My Master and the visitor were engaged in a long talk. My Master was saying, 'Keep him well. Remember he is only a tiger in appearance . . . He is a sensitive soul who understands life and its problems exactly as we do. Take him as a gift from God; only please don't put him in rough company. He is magnificent though he is not at his best now. After a few days of regular feeding at the zoo, he will get back the shine on his coat.'

'We'll take care of that,' the other said.

'Raja, come,' commanded my Master for the last time.

I came out of the shrubberies and covering. The visitor was rather startled at first and remarked, 'Oh, truly the most magnificent of his kind, regal, of grand stature, although you think he is faded. We have our own system of feeding and improving with tonic and he'll be record-breaking. Our zoo can then claim to have the largest tiger for the whole country.'

My master assured him, 'He is quite safe.'

At first sight, I could understand that this man was fearless and used to the company of animals, and had sympathy, and was not another Captain. He asked my Master, 'May I touch him?'

'Yes, certainly,' said my Master, and patted my back. The man came near and stroked my back, and by his touch I could see that I had a friend.

'May we go?' he asked.

My Master said to me, 'Raja, will you come with me?' and I followed him. He opened the cage and said, 'You may get in now, Raja, a new life opens for you. Men, women, and children, particularly children, hundreds of them will come to see you. You will make them happy.' The others got into the jeep to which the cage was yoked. Before we drove off my Master thrust his hand through the bars and whispered to me, 'Both of us will shed our forms soon and perhaps we could meet again, who knows? So goodbye for the present.'

MORE ABOUT PENGUINS,
PELICANS AND PUFFINS

For further information about books available from Penguins please write to Dept EP, Penguin Books Ltd, Harmondsworth, Middlesex UB7 ODA.

In the U.S.A.: For a complete list of books available from Penguins in the United States write to Dept DG, Penguin Books, 299 Murray Hill Parkway, East Rutherford, New Jersey 07073.

In Canada: For a complete list of books available from Penguins in Canada write to Penguin Books Canada Ltd, 2801 John Street, Markham, Ontario L3R 1B4.

In Australia: For a complete list of books available from Penguins in Australia write to the Marketing Department, Penguin Books Australia Ltd, P.O. Box 257, Ringwood, Victoria 3134.

In New Zealand: For a complete list of books available from Penguins in New Zealand write to the Marketing Department, Penguin Books (N.Z.) Ltd, P.O. Box 4019, Auckland 10.

In India: For a complete list of books available from Penguins in India write to Penguin Overseas Ltd, 706 Eros Apartments, 56 Nehru Place, New Delhi 110019.

R. K. Narayan

THE PAINTER OF SIGNS

Raman was considering giving up sign painting (the business was sinking to new levels of meanness in the town) when he met Daisy of the Family Planning Centre. Slender, high-minded, thrillingly independent, Daisy has made up her mind to be modern and is now dedicated to bringing birth control to the people. In such circumstances, Raman's mounting, insistent passion, coupled with Daisy's determination to disregard the messy, wayward concerns of the heart, can only lead to conflict.

R. K. Narayan's magical creation, the city of Malgudi, provides the setting for this wryly funny, bitter-sweet story of love getting in the way of progress.

THE VENDOR OF SWEETS

A widower of firm Gandhian principles, Jagan nonetheless harbours a warmly embarrassed affection for his wastrel son Mali. But even Jagan's patience begins to fray when Mali descends on the sleepy city of Malgudi full of modern notions, with a new half-American wife and a grand plan for selling novel-writing machines . . .

Different generations and different cultures, father and son confront each other and are taken by surprise as this beautifully worked novel unfolds, and as Narayan brings all his delightful genius for comedy into play.

'Narayan wakes in me a spring of gratitude, for he has offered me a second home. Without him I could never have known what it is like to be Indian' – Graham Greene

and

THE MAN-EATER OF MALGUDI

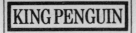
KING PENGUIN

A selection

CARDS OF IDENTITY

Nigel Dennis

A long-empty country mansion is reopened by Captain Mallet, his beautiful second wife and his dashing son Beaufort. Their task is to restore Hyde's Mortimer to its former order in preparation for the summer session of the Identity Club. And their scheme is to persuade various local inhabitants, by employing extremely suspect methods, that they are not really who they think they are. Then the Club meets for the reading of three very bizarre papers . . .

An entertaining and original black comedy which explores the nature of identity and the subtleties of mass persuasion. When it was first published in 1955, *Cards of Identity* drew enormous praise from the critics.

'I have read no novel published during the last fifteen years with greater pleasure and admiration' – W. H. Auden

LEVITATION

Cynthia Ozick

'Ozick's "fictions" are characterized by a bizarre, edgy brilliance and fantastical imagination' – Barbara Trapido in the *Spectator*

Ruth Puttermesser, a New York lawyer, dreams up her own Eden replete with an endless supply of fudge and a steeple of library books . . . A refugee writer analyses Freud by the contents of his rooms in Vienna . . . A photographer pursues her infatuation with her camera, 'her ambassador of desire' . . .

'It is as if Woody Allen had taken over a screen-play by Sholom Aleichem. Zappy prose, a lot to laugh about, a lot to think about' – Sarah Preston in the *Financial Times*

'Ozick has the knack of moving, with impressive speed, in opposite directions at the same time . . . and the whole unlikely rocket takes off, trailing sparks and coloured rain' – Adam Mars-Jones in *The Times Literary Supplement*

A selection

THE STEPDAUGHTER

Caroline Blackwood

'For weeks now I have been sitting in my apartment, which has a panoramic view of the splendours and squalors of Manhattan, and I have been writing letters in my head . . .'

While her absent husband holds Parisian hands by candlelight, 'J', a tense New Yorker in her thirties, writes off her fury in letters about the all-too-present Renata. Her thirteen-year-old stepdaughter is silent, shamefaced, and hopelessly addicted to instant-mix cakes. Renata, evidently, has absolutely nothing to recommend her.

With wit and passion, Caroline Blackwood's irresistible novel locks us into a private hell and then, with a sudden shocking twist, lets us go . . .

'Brilliant . . . An exceptional feat of skill . . . This book demonstrates a major talent' – *The Times*

CHRISTIE MALRY'S OWN DOUBLE-ENTRY

B. S. Johnson

Christie Malry was a simple person. It did not take him long to realize that he had not been born into money. So Christie placed himself next to it by taking a job in a bank and it was there that he encountered the principle of Double-Entry book-keeping. From this he evolved his Great Idea. He realized that life could be expressed in Double-Entry terms: Debit Christie for offence received, credit society for offence given. All accounts were to be settled in full and Christie exacted payment in his own dramatic fashion – with the most alarming consequences.

'Very funny and readable . . . What I admire most in Bryan Johnson's work is its humour and its intelligence – I like his visual jokes, I like his games with the reader, I like his coarseness' – Margaret Drabble

A selection

WHERE I USED TO PLAY ON THE GREEN
Glyn Hughes

Embittered by the death of his wife, William Grimshaw becomes a fanatical evangelist. Creating a terrifying vision of demons and eternal damnation, he struggles to bring the 'barbarous' people of Haworth into total submission to God and ultimately the factory bell. But amidst the fire of conversion he is fighting an inner battle against loneliness and the torment of repressed sexual desire . . .

'Convincing, alarming and memorable. It seems to me a real book, full of truth, vividly imagined and felt' – Ted Hughes in *Arts Yorkshire*

Winner of the *Guardian* Fiction Prize 1982 and the David Higham Prize for fiction 1982

KEEPERS OF THE HOUSE
Lisa St Aubin de Terán

Since the eighteenth century the eccentric and flamboyant Beltrán family have ruled their desolate Andean valley. Now they are almost extinct.

At seventeen, Lydia Sinclair, newly married to Diego Beltrán, the last of the line, arrives at the vast decaying Hacienda La Bebella. As her husband retreats into himself, Lydia takes refuge in learning of his ancestors' tragic history. Benito, the family's oldest retainer, relates tales of splendour and romance, violence and suffering, and from these Lydia weaves a rich Gothic tapestry in which the fantastic legends of the past are mingled with the present necessity for survival in a harsh, drought-ridden land.

'A spellbinding storyteller . . . the book enthrals' – John Mellors in *The Listener*

A selection

O·WHAT A PARADISE IT SEEMS

John Cheever

Skating on Beasley's Pond always makes Lemuel Sears feel nostalgic. He is old enough to wonder – after skating, or when he sees a young couple kissing in the cinema – whether sometime soon he will be exiled from the pleasures of love.

Meanwhile, there is Renée. He first noticed Renée, her style, her splendid and endearing figure, in a New York bank. With her, even in polluted, fast-food, nomad America, the illusion of Paradise lingers. Until he returns to find his free skating-rink turned into a municipal dump. And until . . . But Renée has always said, 'You don't understand the first thing about women.'

'Sheer pleasure . . . his prose is charged like Scott Fitzgerald's' – *Listener*

THE MOONS OF JUPITER

Alice Munro

Alice Munro's women discover, in these eleven stories, that love is rarely honest, kind, or reliable (although they keep trying); that people are not puzzles to be 'arbitrarily solved' (although they continue to search the past and present for clues).

Some are beginning new affairs or leaving threadbare marriages; several inhabit that ambiguous time between youth and middle-age. They want 'new definitions of luck' – less to sweep them off their feet than to help make sense of men, families, relationships and life in their contemporary small-town Canada, mapped by Alice Munro with unerring and unforgettable style.

'Alice Munro has been compared with Proust, short-listed for the Booker Prize, and remains (though dazzling) quite unperturbed and unaffected, her writing smooth and supple' – *Financial Times*

A selection

WAITING FOR THE BARBARIANS

J. M. Coetzee

For decades the Magistrate has run the affairs of a tiny frontier settlement, ignoring the impending war between the barbarians and the Empire, whose servant he is. But when the interrogation experts arrive, he is jolted into sympathy with the victims and into a quixotic act of rebellion which lands him in prison, branded as an enemy of the state.

J. M. Coetzee's second prize-winning novel is an allegory of oppressor and oppressed. Not simply a man living through a crisis of conscience in an obscure place in remote times, the Magistrate is an analogue of all men living in complicity with regimes that ignore justice and decency.

'A remarkable and orginal book' – Graham Greene

'I have known few authors who can evoke such a wilderness in the heart of man . . . Mr Coetzee knows the elusive terror of Kafka' – Bernard Levin

THE CONE-GATHERERS

Robin Jenkins

While the Second World War rages overseas, the life of a large Scottish country estate flows on, lapped by the seasons and enfolded in tradition. Ruled by the equivocal, confused Lady Runcie-Campbell and dominated by Duror the gamekeeper, it seems a world untouched by the tides of destruction.

But as he moves through the forest the brooding figure of Duror undergoes a monstrous transformation. Driven by pent-up love and obsessive hatred to hunt down the small, hunchbacked cone-gatherer, he seeks – and finds – terrible apotheosis.

Written by one of Scotland's finest novelists, *The Cone-Gatherers* is an extraordinary story of violence, lost innocence and sorrow – at its heart the unresolvable mystery of evil, counterpointed by a terrible redemption.

'An exceptional book' – *Scotsman*